"Make love to me, Mason…"

Bailey pressed her lips to his bare chest. "Let's make a beautiful memory together."

"Sweetheart…" His muscles flexed beneath her touch, sending a flash of heat spiraling south.

"I know you want me." Her voice was tinged with sex and sin, and had a strong effect on his resistance.

A growl ripped from his throat. How could Mason deny her—or himself? "There's no turning back after we make love," he managed tightly.

Emotion filled her eyes as she looked up at him. "I know," she whispered, lifting her nightgown over her head.

His mouth went dry and he hardened to the point of pain. "We shouldn't do this," he rasped even as his fingers itched to touch her, explore her intimately.

"But we will," she murmured, easing into his embrace.

He tested the full feminine weight of her breasts, the soft flesh hot and silky in his hands. Then his name fell sweetly from her lips, and Mason was lost.

For tonight, Bailey was his….

Jamie Denton hadn't always dreamed of being a romance author. She planned to attend law school and pursue a career as an attorney—at least until the day she rolled her first sheet of paper into a borrowed typewriter. These days, when she isn't working on her next book, she's a university instructor, sharing her knowledge of the legal system with future legal secretaries.

A Southern California native, Jamie relocated to a small farming community in North Dakota where she lives with her husband, three sons, a menagerie of pets and, for too many months of the year, an inordinate amount of snow. The long winters give her ample time to plot and create her dynamite sexy characters. Look for Jamie's next Temptation novel in 1999!

Books by Jamie Denton

HARLEQUIN SUPERROMANCE
663—THE SECRET CHILD

FLIRTING WITH DANGER
Jamie Denton

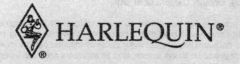

TORONTO • NEW YORK • LONDON
AMSTERDAM • PARIS • SYDNEY • HAMBURG
STOCKHOLM • ATHENS • TOKYO • MILAN • MADRID
PRAGUE • WARSAW • BUDAPEST • AUCKLAND

Thank you to Detective Barnard of the Minot P. D., and
the deputies of the Renville County Sheriff's Department
for sharing the darker side of your jobs, and to
Tim Englebrecht for his undying patience in basic self-
defense. Gentlemen, any mistakes in this book are
definitely mine.

Most importantly, to Janelle Denison and Leslie Furnari.
Thank you for being a part of my life. Because of you,
it's that much richer. And for JoAnn Ross, for believing
when I'd forgotten how. Thank you, my dear friends.

ISBN 0-373-25808-9

FLIRTING WITH DANGER

Copyright © 1998 by Jamie Ann Denton.

1

THE BLOND SIREN, a deadly combination of innocence and sin, teetered dangerously on red stilettos. She looked out of place and scared, damn scared, while she tugged down the hem on the scarlet spandex dress hugging curves that ought to be illegal.

Mason O'Neill drummed his fingers on the steering wheel of his black Ford Bronco and continued to watch her as he'd done for the past two hours. She gripped the lamppost for support, then spoke to one of the regular working girls he recognized from his nightly surveillance. The experienced woman with a well-worn look promised ten minutes of heaven to any man who could cough up twenty bucks. Chuckling to himself, he imagined the kind of education Miss Innocent would gain from that one.

The blonde opened the heavy canvas bag slung over her shoulder and dug through it. Pulling out what looked like a photograph, she flashed it in front of the hooker's face. The seasoned prostitute shook her head and walked away.

Nine years of police work told him the petite blonde, with legs any man could imagine wrapped around him, was no streetwalker. Nor was she his problem, he reminded himself, unless she did something illegal. He doubted that possibility since he'd watched her turn away potential customers for the past two nights.

Miss Innocent sucked in a deep breath. For a brief instant he wondered if she'd end up displaying more of her delicious body than intended. Despite her tawdry outfit, she looked fresh and clean and completely out of her element. Who could someone like her be looking for on the streets of Los Angeles?

He tore his gaze from Goldilocks-Meets-The-Happy-Hooker to search the street for anything unusual. Neon lights cast colorful shadows over the few locals enjoying the sultry warmth of the summer evening. The sounds of raucous laughter and B. B. King drifted onto the street from Shadee's Nite Spot while the "girls" strolled Hollywood Boulevard, hoping to make a buck for a quick roll.

Nothing unusual. Nothing out of the ordinary. And no sign of Devlin Shore or his henchmen.

This was supposed to be his night off, but tailing Shore had become habit. A bad habit he refused to break until he had the slime behind bars. Shore had his fingers in plenty of underhanded and illegal dealings, and the L.A.P.D. had gotten close, but never close enough to make a solid bust. Devlin had always managed to stay one step ahead of them. And Mason swore he wouldn't rest until he had enough evidence to put Shore away for good. And he'd succeed where others had failed in proving the bastard was a cop killer. As far as Mason was concerned, there was a score to settle, which he planned to win. Checkmate.

Miss Innocent moved away from the lamppost

she'd been clinging to, and approached a group of college kids leaving Shadee's. She flashed the photograph in front of them, but they shook their heads and kept moving. Slowly she turned, glancing in his direction. Something twisted in his gut. Guilt? The image of another young innocent flashed through his mind, one he hadn't been able to save. Damn!

The blonde turned, then headed back to her lamppost. He reached for the half-empty pack of cigarettes on the dash, slipped one from the pack and flicked the tip with his finger. After about two seconds' hesitation, he muttered a curse and reluctantly tossed the unlit cigarette through the window. Surveillance was dead work with little to keep his hands or mind busy. Why did he have to try to quit smoking now?

He dragged his gaze back to the blonde in time to see a guy looking for a good time approach her. She shook her head, her hair swaying with the movement. The guy shrugged and moved on, and Miss Innocent visibly sighed. She wobbled slightly, then gripped the post again.

He reminded himself he didn't care, but he couldn't help wondering again what someone like her was doing out on the streets, and who she was looking for. The fact that she continually turned tricks away only increased his curiosity.

Reaching for the disposable cup filled with lukewarm coffee, he kept his eyes on her. She shifted the large canvas handbag, then pushed her hair away from her face. Nothing could alleviate the hot, dry warmth of the California summer, not even the lifting of her hair off her neck and shoulders. When she fanned the back of her neck, Mason shifted in his seat. Her gentle movement was perfectly guileless, but completely feminine and damn erotic.

He'd been alone too long, he thought, consciously resisting the open pack of cigarettes. Too many long nights without a woman to warm his bed and make him forget the job. It didn't matter that nothing could make him forget. Wasn't that why his wife had left him and taken their son with her?

He pushed aside the bitter memories before they could take hold and distract him just as a late-model Mercedes pulled up to the curb a few car lengths away from the blonde. Mason tensed.

The Mercedes door opened and a kid who looked to be eighteen or nineteen stepped out of the car. Mason relaxed. He knew Shore and was familiar with most of his men. This kid wasn't one of them, probably just borrowed Daddy's car and was out looking for a cheap thrill.

He'd give it another hour, then go home and crash for a few before heading into the station. Another night wasted, he thought, slipping the top off the cup. He took a sip of coffee and grimaced, then opened the door and poured the bitter remnants onto the pavement. The all-night diner across the street would satisfy his caffeine habit. Too bad they didn't sell something besides chewing gum to cure his nicotine craving.

He stepped from the Bronco. Watching with amusement as the kid sauntered over to Miss Innocent, he pocketed the keys and shut the door. Fool, he thought. She's not selling.

"Looking for a date, sweetheart?" the kid asked, practically drooling. Mason couldn't really blame him. The blonde wasn't hard on the eyes.

"No, thank you." She smiled politely, then turned away, tugging down the spandex once more and swaying dangerously on her heels.

No, thank you? Mason shook his head. Manners, too.

"Ah, come on," the kid said, reaching out and grabbing hold of her wrist. "I'm new in town and could use some action. I'm a little lonely."

"No," the blonde said. She pulled at her hand, but the kid wouldn't let go.

Mason ground his teeth in frustration. He wasn't in the mood to play knight-in-shining-armor and rescue a misguided damsel in distress. What he wanted was a hot cup of coffee, a cigarette and some sign of Devlin Shore.

"I'll pay you. I'll pay you real good," the kid said, ignoring Miss Innocent's protest.

She tried to pull her hand free again. "You could get arrested for that."

"What are you? A cop?" There was enough of a hint of anger in his voice to make him a threat.

Mason swore under his breath. The department had spent six months trying to establish a believable front Shore couldn't smell this time. Beautiful woman in trouble or not, there was no way he was going to let her blow his cover. If he flashed his badge, word would spread down Hollywood Boulevard faster than a fire fanned by the fierce Santa Ana winds.

"Please, just leave me alone. I'm waiting for someone." Mason heard the panic in Miss Innocent's voice and swore again, more colorfully this time.

"Your waiting days are over, Blondie. I'll take real good care of you." He yanked hard and Miss Innocent stumbled into his arms.

"Leave me alone, please," she said, trying to push away from him.

"Son of a...!" Mason kicked his car door. "Hey, you paying for that?" he yelled at the kid.

"Ah, hell." The kid released her and stepped back.

Mason rounded the Bronco, ignoring the stares of the passersby. "Didn't the boss tell you to stay off the streets tonight?" he said to her. "What are you doing out here? Trying to make a little side money?"

Miss Innocent's jaw fell slack, and she blinked several times. She looked up at the kid, as if weighing which of the two men was the lesser evil.

Mason grabbed hold of her arm before she decided the kid might be the safe bet. "You better thank me, Sugar. If the boss finds out, you know what's going to happen."

He slid his lightweight jacket aside, exposing the gun strapped in his shoulder holster. The kid lifted his hands and took another step back. "Hey, I'm outta here," he said, then jogged over to his car.

She shook her head. "You've got the wrong person." Fear laced a voice sweeter than a song. Her bright blue eyes, innocent eyes, widened.

"It won't work, Sugar," he said, praying he wouldn't regret this act of heroism bordering on stupidity. "Come along quietly, and I won't rat you out—this time." He yanked her arm, and she fell against him.

"Please, let me go." Miss Innocent tried to pull away, but he tightened his grip. Her soft skin felt like satin, and she smelled like a field of daisies. Fresh and innocent, just as he'd imagined.

"I'm telling you, you've got the wrong person. My name's not Sugar, it's Bailey. Bailey Grayson."

Mason ignored her plea and started toward the Bronco. The night was a waste, anyway. He'd take her home and hopefully never have to see her again. "Cute, Sugar, but it won't work," he said, loud enough for the benefit of the small crowd starting to assemble. Then, for her ears only, he whispered, "Come along quietly and don't give me any more trouble."

His height gave him an advantage over Bailey, who barely reached his chin, even in four-inch heels. Those stilts she wore didn't leave her much maneuverability, giving him the upper hand as she wobbled along behind him.

He opened the door. "Get in."

She tried to twist away. He tightened his grip.

"No!" She reached up and grabbed at her heavy canvas bag before swinging her arm back. "I'm not going with you."

His patience, which had never been one of his greatest strengths, was dangerously close to breaking. Not surprisingly, the small crowd had grown. His tenuous patience slipped another notch. "Dammit, get in the truck."

"No!" She swung the heavy bag forward, hitting him square in the chest.

Mason grunted, then cursed. "If you know

what's good for you, you'll get your butt in the truck," he said through clenched teeth.

"I'll scream," she threatened, her panic-filled voice rising.

God, he didn't need this garbage. He should have let the kid have her. But no, he had to go and play hero and save her adorable hide.

He spun her around and pulled her against him, tightening his grip yet again, her backside resting snug against his jean-clad thighs. She pulled in a deep breath in an attempt to expel the scream she'd promised.

"I'm a cop," he growled low in her ear.

She stiffened, the fight going out of her at his declaration. "Oh God."

"Just get in the truck." Opening the door wider, he let go of her.

"Look, I'm not… I mean I didn't—"

"I know," he said before she had the chance to announce her lack of professional intentions. "I'll take you home."

"How do I know you're really a police officer?" she asked warily.

"Get in first, and I'll show you," he told her.

She nodded, then gave him one last look before she climbed into the bucket seat of the Bronco. Red spandex inched up, exposing more of her smooth, tanned thighs. He sucked in a deep breath, then slammed the door. Too bad he couldn't close his thoughts off as easily…because he had a bad feeling those sleek thighs of hers and the sweet scent of daisies were going to keep him awake for more than a few hours.

"OPEN THE GLOVE COMPARTMENT," he ordered, pulling away from the curb. "There's a black leather case with my badge and ID inside."

Bailey did as he asked. She wasn't sure how much trouble, if any, she was in, but the guy was a cop and she sure didn't want to make matters worse by disobeying him.

Sure enough, tucked neatly in the corner of the glove compartment beside a perfectly folded road map and resting atop an envelope labeled in neat script Registration and Insurance, was the little leather case. She pulled it out, opened the flap and looked closely at the identification under the interior lights of the Bronco.

Mason Kieran O'Neill was a thirty-two-year-old Aquarian born on Valentine's Day, six foot four inches tall, two hundred pounds, with brown hair and brown eyes. "Gunshot wound, left thigh" and "tattoo, left arm" were listed under distinguishing marks.

She blew out a breath of relief and slumped back into the seat. Heavens to Betsy, what was she doing? Posing as a prostitute, then climbing into a strange man's truck simply because he said he was a cop, were nothing short of stupid.

"Satisfied?" Detective O'Neill asked.

She glanced in his direction. His eyes weren't really brown, she thought. More gold, like the color of sun-warmed honey. Tiny lines bracketed his eyes, but the look he shot her held little warmth. She had the uncomfortable feeling he knew more about her than she knew about him, regardless of the fact that she'd just learned he'd been shot in the leg and sported a tattoo. A tattoo of what? she wondered briefly.

"Yes." She slipped the ID case back into the glove compartment, then snapped the small door closed. "Thank you," she added, not for producing his identification, but for saving her from the kid in the Mercedes.

He slowed the truck as they approached a traffic signal. He didn't say a word, just turned to stare at her with those hard honey-colored eyes. His hair was combed away from a face that could have been made of granite. And he had a body to match. She knew, since he'd pulled her tight against iron-hard thighs and a wide, muscular chest. He had the body of an athlete, along with the attitude of a barn-sour horse.

"I'm sorry," she said, hating the silence and wishing he'd quit staring at her. "I—I wouldn't have hit you if I'd known you were a police officer."

He returned his attention to the traffic signal, then accelerated when the light turned green. "You're damn lucky I am a cop. Do you have any idea what could have happened to you back there?"

Of course she did. She wasn't a moron. "I didn't break any laws."

He turned off the interior lights, then glanced at her. "Loitering, solicitation. Shall I continue?"

She couldn't argue with the charge of loitering, but solicitation? "I didn't sell anything," she said, pushing aside the panic threatening to engulf her. She hadn't done anything wrong. If he didn't believe her, would he arrest her? How could she call home and tell her mother she'd been hauled off to jail for solicitation? Her mother had enough to worry about.

"What *were* you doing?" he demanded. "Sure as hell not selling Girl Scout cookies."

Bailey ignored the sarcasm. "Looking for someone," she said, then turned to stare out the window. The last word she'd heard from the private detective she'd hired before he'd disappeared was that Leslie had gotten involved with a particularly ruthless individual. Instinct told her the private eye had gotten too close, but what she couldn't understand was how her sister had become involved with someone who indulged in illegal activities. All she knew was that she'd do whatever she had to do to find, and save, her baby sister. This time she wouldn't let Leslie down.

"Who are you looking for?" he asked. He flipped on the turn indicator and pulled up to the curb in front of a New Age shop.

Bailey looked around the nearly deserted, narrow street instead of answering his question. She had no idea where they were or why they'd stopped. Hot-pink neon flashed from the New Age shop, casting eerie shadows throughout the Bronco's interior. Gripping her bag tight against her, she reached for the door handle. Maybe this guy wasn't a cop, after all. Maybe he was some kind of weirdo cop wanna-be with a fake ID.

"Thank you for the ride," she said, and pulled on the handle. "I can walk from here." She gave another tug on the door. Locked! She couldn't believe he'd locked it.

"Look," Detective O'Neill said, turning in the

seat to face her. "Life on the streets isn't pretty. Those girls you were talking to... Do you know what their life is like?"

She could certainly imagine, which was why she was so determined to find her sister.

"They think maybe one or two quick tricks and they'll get the easy cash they need to get by, but before they know it, they're out here every night." O'Neill picked up an open pack of cigarettes and shook one out, tapping it rhythmically against his large palm. She had the feeling the action gave him some sort of comfort.

"You were on the street alone," he said, then slipped the unlit cigarette between his lips, drawing her gaze to his mouth. Such a nice mouth, she thought, then shook her head for even thinking that way about the surly detective.

He pulled the cigarette from his lips and tossed it on the dash with a fierce frown. "You're going to get hurt, Miss Grayson. The world is full of creeps and psychos who would just love to mess up that pretty face of yours, or worse."

"I know what I'm doing," she told him, lifting her gaze to his. There was nothing warm or comforting about his speech, or him, for that matter.

"There are pimps keeping their eye on these girls, on who they talk to. A lot of these girls are hooked on drugs. They'll do just about anything for a fix.... It's not safe here. Go home, kid. Go now before you get into more trouble than you know what to do with."

She knew everything he told her was the truth. Yet hearing him vocalize what her sister could be experiencing evoked a deep fear, and an even deeper desperation to find Leslie.

"I can't go home." She'd promised her mother she'd find Leslie, and she wouldn't return to Wisconsin until she fulfilled that promise. She'd broken too many promises in her twenty-four years, and the people she loved had been hurt.

He shifted his body and slipped the Bronco back into gear. "Okay. There's a homeless shelter not too far from here. I'll take you there."

She shook her head, but realized he was looking at her. "I'm registered at the Commodore Motel on Sunset."

He made a sound that resembled a grunt of disapproval. "By the hour?" he asked, his tone laced with sarcasm.

Bailey gasped. "What do you think I am?"

He shoved the gearshift into park again. Raking his gaze up the length of her legs to the top of the skintight dress, he finally stopped at her heavily made-up eyes. She felt more exposed than if she'd been sitting in his truck without a stitch of clothing.

"It's not what you're thinking," she muttered. The skepticism in his eyes said it all—she looked the part and no doubt she'd been treated the part since she stepped into the most uncomfortable pair of shoes she'd ever worn.

"Then why don't you tell me about it."

She remained silent and turned back to the window. She'd gone to the cops before, and other than filling out a missing-person's report, they hadn't lifted a finger to help her. Her funds were depleting at a rapid-fire pace. She was on her own, and she knew it.

"I thought so," he said, then eased the truck back onto the road.

Five minutes later, Detective O'Neill pulled into the parking lot of the Commodore Motel. Even under the dim streetlights, she could see the peeling paint where many a low-rent rendezvous occurred, but for the past three days she'd called it home. As far as she knew, the carpet didn't move when she turned off the lights, and she'd learned to let the hot water run until the rust disappeared enough for her to shower. Not exactly the Ritz, or her own modern apartment complex in Milwaukee, but the low rates made it affordable.

"Thank you for the ride," Bailey said, and unlocked the door.

She reached for the handle, but the detective stopped her. His big hand upon her shoulder was oddly comforting and warm. She shook off the sensation along with his hand. This man had the power to keep her from her goal, and she'd be a fool to think otherwise. The cops had been no help, and O'Neill was one of *them*.

"If I see you on the streets again, I'll run you in." His voice was hard, as hard as that body of his.

"Don't worry, Detective," she said in her iciest tone, resenting his interference. "You won't see me again. I'll make sure of it."

She ignored the warning in his eyes and opened the door. Slipping from the truck, she jerked the hem of her skirt down before her feet hit the pavement. As she carefully picked her way around the cracks in the parking lot, she fished in her bag for the key to her room, resisting the urge to look over her shoulder to see if he was watching her.

Unlocking the door, she slipped into the room without turning on the lights. After tossing her bag on the bed, she kicked off the killer shoes and wiggled out of the tight spandex, then headed for the shower.

The overhead light flickered, then hummed to life, illuminating the dull green tiled bathroom in a harsh fluorescent glow. She slipped off the rest of her clothes and turned on the shower.

Damn, she thought. An overzealous detective out to save her from herself, ruining her plans, was the last thing she needed. Well, she'd have to come up with a disguise of some sort. A wig ought to do the trick, and a new outfit. No doubt Dick Tracy would recognize the red spandex, especially after he'd practically stripped her of it with his eyes.

She ignored the fluttering in her belly *that* thought caused and stepped beneath the hot spray. A quick shower and a good night's sleep and she'd be ready to face another night of lecherous stares and crude remarks. And maybe, with a little luck, she'd finally catch Devlin Shore's attention.

2

BAILEY ADJUSTED the strap of her new white satin garter belt, courtesy of Frederick's of Hollywood, then secured the tops of inexpensive white lace leggings with the fastenings from the garters, wondering how on earth anyone could possibly go out in public dressed like this. She turned and looked over her shoulder at the cracked mirror, frowning at the sight of her derriere barely covered in a pair of denim cutoffs that made Daisy Duke appear modest in comparison. She shook her head. What a scandal she'd cause back home if she dared to stroll down Main Street wearing this getup.

She turned around to face the mirror again, and with a critical eye, examined her appearance. If only the partners in her staid accounting firm could see her now, she thought with a grimace. Even her own mother wouldn't recognize her beneath the short dark wig and heavy makeup. Dick Tracy shouldn't, either—she hoped.

Relatively satisfied that Detective O'Neill wouldn't bother her tonight, she pulled on the imitation-leather boots she'd found in a thrift store that afternoon, then cuffed them over her knee. With one last adjustment to the hot-pink crop-top that exposed more than it covered, she slung her bag over her shoulder and headed out the door.

Twenty minutes later, she rounded the corner onto Hollywood Boulevard, grateful for the lower-heeled boots. After a quick scan of the street, she let out the pent-up breath she'd been holding. Certain she saw no sign of the detective's Bronco, or him, she started toward Shadee's Nite Spot, the place she'd learned Devlin Shore frequented.

Hollywood Boulevard was hopping with activity Friday night with a mixture of tourists and street people. She passed a woman dressed much like herself on the arm of a burly guy wearing grease-stained denim and a faded blue T-shirt. *Business as usual*, she thought as she strolled toward the strain of blues coming from Shadee's.

A sleek gunmetal gray Mercedes idling in front of the late-night spot caught her attention. A dark tinted window rolled down and someone tossed a cigarette onto the pavement. The door opened. Bailey stopped a few car lengths away and leaned against a storefront window, watching as a tall man wearing a business suit emerged from the car. With his thick black hair pulled into a ponytail, emphasizing a square jaw and deep-set eyes, she couldn't say he was an unattractive man, but he gave her the creeps. He spoke to one of the prostitutes she thought she'd seen the night before. Bailey wasn't close enough to hear their conversation, but the menacing quality of the man's voice sent a shiver racing down her spine.

The woman shook her head and said something. She looked frightened, and Bailey couldn't blame her. The guy wearing the expensive, well-cut suit looked mean…and familiar.

Survival instinct told her to keep going and not

pay them any attention. Gut instinct told her this was Devlin Shore, and the man knew where she could find her sister.

What the hell was wrong with her? Why was she hesitating? Because, as much as she hated to admit it, she was scared. This was what she'd been waiting for—the chance to catch Shore's attention. She had to get him to notice her, and like what he saw, so he'd offer to "protect" her.

She took a deep breath, trying to figure out what to say, keeping her gaze locked on the pair. She took a few hesitant steps forward. Shore. She'd seen his photograph in the newspapers, and the resemblance was just too close, it had to be him.

He grabbed the woman and shoved her toward the rear of the vehicle. The woman stumbled, and he gave her arm a rough yank, causing her to cry out. A wave of anger washed over Bailey. No one deserved to be treated like that.

He waved something in the woman's face, but she couldn't tell what—until the object caught the light from the street lamp above. Bailey's mouth went dry. He had a knife. In the middle of the busy street, he was waving a lethal-looking knife.

Ignoring the possible consequences, she headed in the direction of Shore's vehicle. If anyone had told her she'd approach a man with a knife while she was dressed like a prostitute, she'd have told them they were crazy. Now she was the one who was crazy, because that's exactly what she intended to do.

Someone fell into step beside her. Bailey turned, ready to give the guy the brush-off, but the words died in her throat when she looked into the angry face of Detective Mason O'Neill.

"Shut up and keep walking." His low voice was filled with authority.

"Dammit! How did you recognize me?"

"Just keep walking, Miss Grayson, and try not to draw attention to yourself."

She nearly laughed. She was dressed so she *would* draw attention.

As they neared Shore and the woman, O'Neill slung his arm around her shoulders and pulled her against him, as if he guessed her intent to approach the man. Damn him. When she'd looked in the mirror, she'd hardly recognized herself. She never dreamed he'd be able to spot her.

Something dug into her side and she tried to move away. His arm clamped tighter around her, keeping her lodged against him. Heat emanated from him, and his hold around her shoulders was like a steel band. She shifted, and felt the outline of his shoulder holster pressed against her.

Living amidst men wielding knives, women peddling their flesh in the name of free enterprise and dealing with surly detectives was light-years away from farm life in Whitewater, Wisconsin, or even her secure world in Milwaukee. She felt as if she was trapped in the middle of a bad B movie, and she'd been cast in the starring role.

She tried to push away from him, but he pulled her closer. "Where are you taking me?" she whispered when they passed Shore and the woman.

He remained silent, infuriating her. Damn this man and his intrusion. With his grip on her, escape was impossible, at least not without causing a scene. When they reached the corner, he turned and led her toward a blue sedan.

"Where are you taking me?" she demanded again. She was getting a little tired of his high-handedness. First, he lectures her on the perils of a life of prostitution, threatens her, scares the life out of her, then he forces her to take a walk with him, ruining her plans.

He stopped in front of the sedan, then reached into his back pocket. Bailey stared at the shiny handcuffs he produced, wondering if he was merely going to threaten her again, or if he'd really arrest her as he'd promised.

"You have the right to remain silent," he said, grabbing her arm and slapping the cuff around her wrist. Stunned, she didn't argue when he turned her around and slipped the bag from her shoulder before snapping the other cuff on her free hand.

"You can't be serious!" She'd never been hand-cuffed in her life. Never been arrested. Never even had so much as a speeding ticket.

"You have the right to an attorney." He opened the rear passenger door to the sedan. She felt his hand on the top of her head as he guided her into the vehicle.

She sat in the back of the unmarked car, stunned. This couldn't be happening to her. She hadn't done anything wrong.

"If you can't afford an attorney—"

"I know. One will be appointed to represent me." She looked up at Detective O'Neill. One arm rested on the hood of the car, and he leaned toward her. Those eyes she'd thought resembled warm honey less than twenty-four hours ago now held more than a hint of anger. What did he have to be angry about? She was the one who'd been trussed up like a rodeo calf.

She offered him her most condescending smile. "Can I ask what the charge is, Detective?"

"Stupidity," he said. "For starters." He slammed the door on her and her derision.

MASON SLIPPED behind the wheel, trying to keep a straight face, but the angry hissing coming from the handcuffed woman in the back seat of the sedan was almost too much for him. No doubt about it, Miss Innocent was fuming. He'd warned her, and she chose to ignore that warning. As far as he was concerned, she had no one to blame but herself for her current state of confinement.

She kicked at the seat in front of her. "I demand you release me," she railed, then added another kick. "Immediately."

Mason started the car and pulled away from the curb. "Keep it up, and I'll add assaulting a police officer to the charges." He glanced in the rearview mirror in time to see her narrowed gaze boring into him.

The look in her eyes was pure venom. "Go ahead. Then at least you'd have something real to charge me with."

He ignored her sarcasm and turned his attention back to the heavy traffic. What he really wanted to do was read her the riot act for being so damn stupid. Even a fool could see she intended to intervene and confront Shore. The gleam of determination in her cornflower blue eyes had made his blood run cold. Why, he wasn't sure, but he chose to ignore that, as well.

She was up to something. Despite her lady-of-the-evening attire, she was no prostitute. What he wanted to know was *who* was she looking for, and if that someone was indeed Devlin Shore. He always trusted his instincts. Those same instincts were telling him there was a connection between Bailey Grayson and Shore. He'd stake his badge on it.

By the time he pulled into the rear of the station, his prisoner was still shooting him heated looks in the rearview mirror. He couldn't help admiring the way her eyes sparkled when she was angry. He shoved that thought aside. He'd spent enough hours tossing and turning during the long nights as it was. The last thing he needed was to add fuel to the testosterone fire that thoughts of Bailey Grayson caused.

He parked the car and shut off the ignition. Turning to face her, he casually rested his arm over the back of the seat. Fifteen minutes hadn't cooled her temper any, he noticed.

"This is so stupid," she said, then stomped her foot on the floorboard. "I demand that you release me."

A smile tugged at his mouth. God, she was an exciting mixture of innocence and sensuality. It had been a long time since a woman had affected him, but he'd be damned if he'd let this one interfere with his job. They were close to nailing Shore, and once his job was done, he planned to pack it in and move back to Chicago to be near his son.

"Are you giving up your right to remain silent?"

"Oh?" She cocked her head to the side. The short dark wig swayed with the movement, brushing against her cheek. "You mean I have rights?" she asked sarcastically.

"Everyone has rights," he said, resisting the urge to yank that wig from her head and let those long blond tresses fall free.

She lifted her chin, a move filled with defiance emphasizing a stubborn streak a mile wide. "There is no such thing, you know. You can't arrest me for stupidity."

"I already have."

"I can sue you for false arrest. You can't arrest someone without probable cause, and I haven't done anything wrong."

"I've got plenty of probable cause, Miss Grayson."

"You do not!"

"How does solicitation sound?"

Her eyes narrowed, and he was struck again by how adorable she looked when she was fired up.

"Like a crock," she retorted. "I didn't do anything wrong."

"Maybe probable cause is the wrong word choice." He leaned farther into the seat. "How about criminal intent?"

"Intent? I had no intention of committing a crime."

He turned and unsnapped his seat belt. "We can let the lawyers fight it out. I've got all the time in the world."

"Look, you—"

He stepped from the vehicle and slammed the door on her and her tirade. Crossing his arms, he rested his backside against the car, giving her a minute to get it out of her system. When she calmed down, he'd take her inside and discover exactly what she was up to—because innocent of any real crime or not, Bailey Grayson was already in trouble.

BAILEY TOOK a deep breath trying to still the wild beating of her heart and the fear threatening to choke her. What was she going to do? She didn't have enough money to post bail, and she didn't have a clue how much *stupidity*, or even the more serious charge of solicitation, was going to cost her. Just the thought of calling her already worried mother was enough to make her think that a night in jail wouldn't be all that bad.

She could hear Detective O'Neill's tuneless whistling as he leaned against the sedan, as if he indeed had all the time in the world to torture her. Okay, she amended. Torture wasn't exactly true, but it was close to what she was feeling.

She leaned back against the cheap, vinyl seat and stared up at the headliner. O'Neill couldn't have ruined her one and only chance at Devlin Shore. She was certain Shore had seen her with O'Neill. They knew cops on the streets, and someone with as much presence as O'Neill would have to be known as a cop—especially by a man as allegedly powerful as Shore. An alternate plan had to be formulated. Biting her lower lip, she wondered if Shore would believe her if she simply told him the truth—that she'd been busted. There was the slightest chance it could work.

O'Neill opened the door and rested his forearm

on the roof of the car. He leaned forward and she caught his scent, spice and man. "Calmed down?" he asked in a reasonable tone that set her teeth on edge.

She looked at him. The anger she'd seen earlier had been replaced by a look of indifference. She wasn't fooled. She might not know Mason O'Neill well, but she had a feeling the last thing this man could be accused of was indifference, about anything.

"I suppose," she said. "I still don't think you can arrest me."

"That's your opinion."

He clamped his hand around her upper arm and helped her out of the car. An odd fluttering started in her belly that worried her. The same thing had occurred last night when he'd touched her. She squelched that idea and remembered she hadn't had anything to eat since her mad shopping spree for tasteless and tacky apparel that afternoon. Oh, well, she thought, at least she'd get three hots and a cot if he really was going to throw her butt in the slammer.

She tried not to let that thought depress her as O'Neill led her toward a gray metal door, where he pushed a large red button on the white stucco wall. Seconds later, a buzz sounded and he swung the door open and guided her down a long hallway with beige walls and an old speckled linoleum floor. The place smelled of strong disinfectant, which made her nose wrinkle. She expected ringing telephones with a crush of people rushing back and forth, but the only sounds she heard were the click of her boots upon the floor and the jangle of keys somewhere in the distance.

They reached the end of the hallway, and he guided her to the left and through another door into a room filled with desks overflowing with papers, files and an assortment of personal effects. Without a word, they passed a table with a coffee machine that looked as if it hadn't had a decent cleaning since it was purchased, nor, apparently, had the variety of stained coffee mugs surrounding it. A pink bakery box lay open, and she peeked inside and grimaced at the stale and shriveled chocolate doughnut covered with sprinkles.

Finally, he stopped at one of the overflowing desks, where he gently turned her around. "If you promise to behave yourself, I'll take off the cuffs."

She nodded, then waited patiently for him to fulfill his promise. He did, and she rubbed her aching wrists.

"Sit down," he ordered.

Bailey did as he told her for fear that he'd slap those confining wrist bracelets on her again.

"Coffee?" he asked, slipping out of his jacket.

She thought about those stained mugs and the filthy coffeemaker. "No. Thank you."

He shrugged, then gave her one of those hard looks she'd come to associate with him that clearly said she'd better not move. He didn't have to worry. She wasn't going anywhere. Maybe if she cooperated he'd eventually release her. Although she had to admit, her intuitive skills as far as O'Neill went had thus far been severely lacking. Still, she could hope. Just as she still believed in her chances of running into Devlin Shore and finding her sister. At the moment, her immediate social calendar was empty, so she might as well play along and see what O'Neill had in mind. Besides, maybe he could help her.

Before she could formulate a plan on just how he might be able, or even willing, to help her, he sauntered across the room toward two detectives in front of a computer. He motioned to them with the mug of steaming coffee in hand, then propped his hip against another ugly metal desk. He spoke low so she couldn't hear him, but the other detectives glanced her way and nodded.

A prick of nervous apprehension climbed up her spine. She had no idea what was going on, but she had a feeling that before the night was over, O'Neill would no doubt inform her, along with another of his threats.

He straightened and headed in her direction. Under the glare of fluorescent light, he looked even larger than he had the night before. He was trim, but muscular, which she knew from firsthand experience. He wore a pair of jeans faded to white in all the right places, and a loose-fitting knit shirt that did nothing to hide the wide breadth of his chest and shoulders. She wondered if he had a light sprinkling of hair on his chest, then quickly chastised herself for being foolish. Whether or not O'Neill had a furry chest was none of her concern. Her objective was to locate her sister and return her to Wisconsin. Neither she nor Leslie could afford to have her clouding the issues with thoughts of chest hair.

After setting his mug on a coffee-ring stain, he hooked his foot around the army-issue chair and pulled it out, then straddled the seat. He shifted, adjusting his shoulder holster, then folded his arms and rested them on the back of the chair. When he looked at her with those intense eyes, she almost forgot she was furious with him for ruining her plans. Almost.

"You want to tell me what you were doing tonight?"

She sucked in a deep breath. "I was…" What? Trying to get inside Shore's organization in hopes of locating Leslie? Trying to assuage her own guilt?

"I'm waiting."

She looked at O'Neill. There was nothing soft or compassionate about the man. How would he ever understand that she felt responsible for Leslie's current predicament? How could she make him see that she had to find Leslie and try to help her, to give her back the time that had been stolen from her? Was there any way at all to let him know that if she hadn't been so busy trying to shake the small-town image, she, or Leslie, wouldn't be here?

"It's a long story," she finally said. An old telefax machine in the corner started to wheeze and rattle like a steam engine. One of the detectives, a portly fellow with graying hair and wire-rimmed glasses too small for his large face, pushed out of his chair and headed toward the machine.

"And I have all night." O'Neill reached for his coffee and took a sip, watching her over the rim. "Why don't you start by telling me your connection to Devlin Shore."

"Hey, O'Neill. You might want to see this," the portly detective called over his shoulder. "Sounds like one that belongs to your boy." He ripped the sheet from the telefax then dropped it on O'Neill's desk on his way back to his own.

O'Neill set his mug back on the coffee stain, picked up the rolled paper, then opened it like an ancient scroll. His dark eyebrows puckered. "Son of a..." He stood abruptly, dropping the paper back on the desk. "Don't move." He turned to the two detectives. "Keep an eye on her," he barked before stalking out of the room.

Bailey glanced over at the detectives. They sat huddled together looking at the computer on the portly fellow's desk. Wondering what upset O'Neill, she reached for the rolled sheet, keeping her eyes locked on the men. They didn't pay her any attention, and for an instant, she considered walking out of the room. They were so engrossed in the computer, she doubted they'd even notice.

Better not. With her luck, O'Neill would track her down and really do something nasty, like charge her with resisting arrest.

Trying to keep as quiet as possible, she started to unroll the yellowish sheet of paper. The words *Cause of Death: Probable Homicide* caught her attention, and she shivered.

She shouldn't be surprised. After all, she was in a police station and homicide was an everyday part of life for law enforcement officials. She preferred her days filled with neat columns of numbers. Numbers were predictable. One and one always equaled two, which was just the way she liked it.

She finished unrolling the fax and started reading. "Oh, God. No." A young girl, thought to be a minor, had been found murdered.

She tried to ignore the loud buzz in her ears as

she searched for a physical description of the girl. "Please, God, no," she whispered. The victim was approximately fifteen to seventeen years of age, Caucasian with blond hair. No identification found on or near the body.

Her hands began to shake, until slowly her entire body followed suit. She felt cold, so damn cold. Someone stepped into her line of vision, and she looked up to find O'Neill. With a frown pulling his eyebrows together, large hands braced against lean hips and feet spread wide apart, he looked like a warrior. Or a dark angel.

"You're as white as a sheet," he said, but his voice sounded far away. "Miss Grayson? Bailey? Are you all right?"

She shook her head and lifted the yellow paper toward him. The buzzing in her ears increased and her vision began to narrow, shading everything but O'Neill in a dull gray. She swayed in the chair. "It's her."

"Who?" His voice echoed through her mind, strong and sure. She tried to concentrate on that voice, on that strength, but felt herself slipping farther into the gray tunnel where only a pinpoint of light remained.

"It's my sister," she managed to say, seconds before the light extinguished.

3

MASON CAUGHT HER an instant before her eyes fluttered closed. Ignoring the curious stares from Parker and Jamison, he scooped Bailey into his arms and carried her into the lieutenant's office, which was empty. She weighed less than his hundred-and-ten-pound German shepherd, and her skin felt twice as soft as cashmere. He kicked the door shut with his foot, then gently laid her on the leather sofa.

He returned to his desk and picked up the fax she'd dropped when she'd fainted. Was it possible she was right—this latest homicide was her sister? He suspected Shore's involvement. Could Bailey Grayson have also?

He returned to Forbes's office, found a blanket in the file cabinet and tucked it around her. If she was in shock, she'd probably start shaking again when she came to. Keeping her body warm was important.

He crossed the office and dropped into the lieutenant's chair. Picking up the phone, he dialed Blake Hammond's home number, hoping his partner was in his own bed tonight. With Blake, it was hard to tell. By the third ring, Mason was ready to give up.

"Yeah?" Blake's voice sounded scratchy and sleepy.

"You'd better leave a twenty on the nightstand, loverboy, and kiss the flavor-of-the-week good-bye," Mason said. "We've got a problem."

"Shore?" Blake asked, sounding fully awake now.

"I'm pretty certain. And this one's young." He looked over at Bailey, who'd begun to stir. He wasn't the least bit remorseful that he'd brought her into the station. She'd been headed straight for Shore. It could have been her body that had been found. For her sake, he hoped the homicide wasn't her sister. Even if it wasn't, if Shore had her... "I think I've got her sister in Forbes's office."

"This the same sweet young thing you been telling me about?"

"One and the same." He dragged his gaze away with more reluctance than he thought possible. Becoming involved wasn't his style, and he couldn't find any reason why Bailey Grayson got to him. She wasn't his type. He didn't go for sunshine and sweet. He liked his women willing and experienced, not that he'd had any lately, but that's what he wanted. The fact that he found her attractive irritated him. He had a job to do, plain and simple. He couldn't afford distractions—no matter how enticing.

"I take it there's a connection," Blake said.

"Would I be calling you at midnight if there wasn't?" Mason complained.

"Settle down, pal. I'll see you in twenty."

The line went dead before Mason could reply. He'd been working with Blake since the death of his previous partner, Jim Evers, nearly three years ago. Blake was good, and they were close. Close, and gaining more ground every day in building an airtight case against Shore. He figured another three to four weeks tops, and they'd have the cop-killing bastard right where they wanted him.

He placed another call, this one to the coroner to see if they had photographs of the victim ready to be sent over. He didn't like the thought of taking Bailey to the morgue to identify the body. The alternative was for him to obtain a photo ID and compare it to the photograph he'd seen her parading in front of anyone who would look.

Once the coroner's office promised to send over the photographs, he hung up and crossed the room again to sit on the edge of the sofa. He checked Bailey's pulse, which was strong. The cold, clammy feeling had left her skin. The black wig did nothing to hide her beauty. Even the gaudy makeup job couldn't hide her innocence. Thick, mascara-covered lashes fanned against cheeks as smooth as porcelain. Gently, he brushed the dark hair from her face and cupped her cheek in his palm. Her skin was so damn soft.

Her lashes fluttered and he found himself looking into her pain-filled, cornflower gaze. He stood suddenly and turned away, disgusted with himself and the protective instincts he felt toward her. Dammit, someone had to protect her, she sure wasn't going to do it. The only thing he couldn't understand was why it had to be him.

"O'Neill?"

"Yeah." He kept his back to her. He couldn't stand to see the look in her eyes.

"Is it her? Is it Leslie?"

"I don't know yet," he answered truthfully. "The coroner's office is sending over more information. We'll have to wait."

She began to cry, soft sobs that tugged at a heart he'd thought was encased in steel. He had to get out of there, and fast, before he did something really stupid, like take her in his arms and hold her. "I'll be back," he muttered, then left her alone in Forbes's office.

Twenty minutes later, when Blake Hammond and Lieutenant Forbes walked into the station, Mason wasn't feeling any better.

"I figured he'd want to be here," Hammond said, indicating the senior officer. "It'll save us a truckload of paperwork later." Blake glanced toward Forbes's office, then back at Mason, lifting a questioning eyebrow. Mason chose to ignore Blake.

"What's up, O'Neill?" Forbes said, crossing the room to his office. He stopped at the door and turned to give Mason a hard look. "You'd better have a damn good reason why you've got a hooker in there."

"She's not a working girl, Lieutenant," Mason said, following Blake and their superior into the cramped office. Blake took a seat, and Mason snapped the miniblinds shut, then leaned against the door, where he could keep an eye on Bailey.

Forbes gave him a distrustful expression, then glared at Bailey. "Who are you?"

"Bailey Grayson." She'd stopped crying and sat stiffly on the sofa, gripping the edge of the seat. The wig was gone, her own hair floating around her shoulders like a golden cloud. Mason itched to touch it, to let the gold strands sift through his fingers. He crossed his arms, instead.

"What are you doing here?" Forbes demanded, dropping into the chair behind his desk.

"I'm not sure," she said, then looked to Mason.

"You'd better have a good reason, O'Neill," Forbes repeated. "Or did Hammond wake up my whole damn household so you can show me what you found tonight?"

"Lieutenant," Blake said in that calm, reasoning tone he'd perfected, "the girl is connected to Shore."

That got Forbes's attention, and he settled his dark gaze on Mason. "Connected how?"

"I don't know yet."

Forbes expelled an impatient breath. "What *do* you know, O'Neill?"

"I got a fax from downtown." Mason pulled the paper from his hip pocket and tossed it onto Forbes's desk. The lieutenant picked it up and started to read.

"A couple of patrol officers found the body of a young girl," Mason continued. "Approximately fifteen to seventeen years of age in an alley off Vine, suspected prostitute. Miss Grayson believes it could be her sister. My guess is the sister has been employed by Shore." He looked to Bailey for confirmation. When she nodded, a heavy weight settled in his stomach.

Blake reached for the fax once the lieutenant finished reading. "Do you know for certain if the victim is one of Shore's girls?"

Mason shook his head. "Not yet."

"Witnesses?" Forbes asked, his tone more reasonable.

"None, sir."

"Any evidence," Blake asked, not looking up from the fax, "besides the gunshot wound to the chest?" He looked at the lieutenant. "No exit wound."

"Good." Forbes reached for the phone. "At least we can have ballistics check it out."

Forbes placed the call to ballistics with an order to notify him as soon as the type of weapon was determined. He replaced the receiver, then nodded in Bailey's direction. "How did she get here?"

Mason straightened. "I arrested her."

Forbes gave him that skeptical look again. "I thought you said she wasn't a prostitute!"

"She's not."

"Then what did you arrest her for?"

"For intending to make a stupid mistake."

Blake laughed. Too bad Forbes didn't find any humor in the situation.

"I ought to send you packing back to patrol, O'Neill. You've been a burr on my backside too long. You can't arrest a citizen for being stupid."

"She was about to approach Shore," Mason explained. He didn't bother to tell his superior officer that the thought of Bailey anywhere near a man like Devlin Shore turned his blood to ice and his temper to fire. How could he explain something he didn't understand himself?

Forbes stood slowly and rounded the desk. He hitched his hip against the Formica top, bracing his hands behind him. "You'd better start at the beginning, O'Neill, because as far as I'm concerned, you're in it deep this time."

"He was only doing his job, sir."

All three men turned to stare at Bailey. She kept the blanket tucked around her, probably because she felt uncomfortable dressed as she was in front of three strangers.

Forbes sent a quelling look in her direction. "Would somebody please tell me what the hell is going on?"

Blake rose and left the room, coming back with a glass of water.

"Thank you," she said, offering him a weak smile before taking the glass. She took a sip, then held the glass with trembling fingers.

She looked up at the lieutenant, and Mason's gut tightened at the pain shimmering in her eyes. That damn protective urge struck him again, but he couldn't push it aside.

She cleared her throat. "Six weeks ago my sister ran away from home. Why isn't important right now. What is important is that I discovered she was under the influence of a man named Devlin Shore."

Blake turned his chair around to face her. "How do you know that, Ms. Grayson?"

Bailey took another sip of water the younger detective had brought her. She'd recounted this story numerous times and no one had been willing to help her. Thinking that perhaps this time would be different, and she could get the help she needed to find Leslie, she told them what they wanted to know. "When my sister ran away, my mother and I both thought she would come to me in Milwaukee. That's where I live. I'm an accountant with Miller and Fitzgerald."

She looked at O'Neill, expecting to see disbelief on his face. He showed no emotion whatsoever about that little detail of her life. "Anyway," she said, turning her attention back to the lieutenant, "when Leslie never arrived, I hired a private detective to locate her. The last time I heard from him, he told me that my sister had been seen with Devlin Shore. It's possible she's working for him."

"Not in the kind of job that pays taxes," Mason grumbled.

"I *have* to find my sister," she said, feeling the old frustration rising to the surface again. "I figured if I pretended to be a…a…"

"Working girl," the younger detective supplied in a calm, soothing voice. She imagined he must be very good at interrogating suspects. He had the finely chiseled, classical features of a Greek god, lacking the hard-edged look of O'Neill. The younger detective's soft gray eyes were warm and inviting, making him appear approachable, as if you'd want to confide in him and tell him all your secrets. He had a polished look and, she suspected, was pretty much a lady killer when he smiled. Even his thick raven black hair was neatly trimmed and styled, unlike O'Neill's short-cropped hair that looked finger combed most of the time.

"Yes," she said. "If I can lure Shore, I can find Leslie, then get her safely back home."

No one spoke. They just stared at her as if she'd lost her mind. That nervous tingling was back in the pit of her stomach again, so she took another sip of water in hopes of settling it.

"That's a pretty harebrained idea, Ms. Grayson," the lieutenant finally said, his thick, salt and pepper brows pulled together in a straight line. "How long have you been doing this?"

She set the glass aside and pushed her hair out of her face. She glanced over at O'Neill, but he simply stood in front of the door with his arms crossed. "Three days," she told them, trying to ignore O'Neill. "I've taken a leave of absence until I can find her."

The lieutenant pushed off the desk, shoved his hands in the pockets of his navy slacks and paced in front of her. He lacked the height of O'Neill, but was no less intimidating. "You're a very brave woman, Ms. Grayson," he said, the heavy timber of his voice equal to the craggy lines deepening his veteran weary face. "Not too bright, but no one ever said you needed brains to be brave."

O'Neill moved away from the door to sit on the arm of the sofa. "You can go back to dairy country," he said. "We'll handle it from here."

She ignored the roughness in his voice. She wasn't leaving until her sister was safely beside her. "What about the girl found tonight?"

"We don't know that it is your sister," the lieutenant said.

"You don't know that it isn't, either," she argued.

The lieutenant stopped pacing to stare at her. "Are you up to identifying the body, Ms. Grayson?" His blue-green eyes held none of the compassion she'd sensed earlier from him.

"I have to. I have to be sure it isn't her."

"No, you don't." O'Neill moved, retrieving her

bag from behind the desk. "She's got a photograph of her sister," he said to the others, handing her the bag.

She dug out Leslie's high-school picture. "How do you know that?" she said.

His lips curved into something that resembled a grin, but she couldn't be sure. "I watched you flash it around the past two nights."

He held out his hand for the picture, then left the small office.

Bailey fought the urge to follow him, to see for herself that it wasn't Leslie, but a part of her was grateful for O'Neill's handling of the situation. She'd never fainted before tonight, but obviously everyone had their limits. No doubt about it, she was certainly getting close to the breaking point.

O'Neill came back into the room, a color photocopy and Leslie's photograph in his hand. He didn't look in her direction, increasing her nervousness. "What do you think?" he asked the other men, setting the photos on the desk. "Blake?"

"Not even close," Blake answered, then turned to face her. "It's okay, Ms. Grayson. It's not your sister."

Relief flooded through her at his words. "Are you sure?" she asked.

"Positive," O'Neill said. "Now, will you let us handle this?"

The lieutenant examined the photographs, then, seemingly satisfied, handed her back the picture of Leslie.

"I'm not leaving," she told him. "You might as well lock me up, O'Neill, because it's the only way you'll keep me from finding Leslie."

Mason turned and gave her a hard look. "Listen up, country girl. If I find you so much as within fifty feet—"

Blake stood and rested his hand on Mason's shoulder. "I think we can use her."

"Come again?"

"I think we can use her," Blake said. "She's just the type Shore goes for."

Mason looked at his partner as if he was crazy. Blake knew about Ashley Adams. The entire department knew about the plant that had gone sour nearly three years ago. How could he even suggest they use another civilian as a lure? "No way," he said. "No way in hell."

"What would I have to do?" Bailey asked, not distressed in the least by Blake's suggestion.

"What you've been doing," Blake said. "Get Shore's attention, then when he makes you an offer you can't refuse, you accept."

She stood, the blanket sliding down her half-naked body. "I'll do whatever it takes."

Mason stooped to pick up the blanket, then laid it over her shoulders, hoping she'd take the hint and cover those long legs and all that exposed skin that was making his temperature rise. "No, she won't."

"Yeah, I think she will," Forbes said, dropping into the chair behind his desk. "It's not the first time we've used civilians, O'Neill. She's been doing it on her own, and this time she'd have the protection of the department."

"It's a good idea, Mason," Blake said. "Kate Morgan has had too much street exposure in vice. Besides, if Ms. Grayson's been spotted by Shore already, things will happen a lot faster than if we found a fresh plant."

But at least a female undercover officer was a trained professional. Using a civilian was just too damn risky. Mason shook his head. "It's too dangerous." The nightmare was happening again. He wouldn't let it, because there was no way he was going to allow her to be dragged into this any more than she already was. He'd hauled her into the station to keep her from getting herself killed. The last thing he wanted on his conscience was intentionally putting her in front of Devlin Shore. If Shore so much as suspected she was a plant, there'd be nothing left of her for Mason to protect.

"She'll be wired," Blake argued.

So had Ashley.

She placed her hand on his arm and looked up at him with determination shimmering in her blue gaze. "I *want* to do it," she said, her voice soft.

"I'm against this," he told her. "You could get killed."

"You won't let that happen, O'Neill," she said.

There was no challenge in her voice, only sheer determination, and a trust he didn't deserve. Ashley had trusted him, and what had it gotten her? Trust? He nearly laughed. Not something to be given to Mason O'Neill, cop with a score to settle.

Forbes reached for something across his desk. "Tomorrow I'll get Kate Morgan to help prep Ms. Grayson." He jotted something on a yellow legal pad, then looked over at Bailey. "Kate's been working on the Shore case from the beginning. She's a good cop, and she'll help brief you."

"Where are you staying, Ms. Grayson?" Blake asked.

"The Commodore Motel," Mason said, ignoring the sharp look from Lieutenant Forbes. "She can stay with me until we're finished with her."

"Won't work," Blake said, rubbing his chin. "If we can get her close enough, Shore could have her watched."

"Then find us a place," Mason demanded. "I'm not leaving her alone. If she's that important to the department, they can foot the bill."

Forbes threw his pen on the desk and stood. "Now look here, O'Neill—"

"Lieutenant, he's right," Blake said in that placating tone of his. "This isn't your average perp we're after."

Forbes took a deep breath, and Mason figured the lieutenant was counting to ten, something he usually did whenever they were around each other. "All right," he finally said. "Set it up, Hammond." He gave Mason a warning look. "Screw this up, O'Neill, and you'll be marking tires and handing out parking tickets until retirement."

THERE WAS ONLY one thing Mason could do now that Blake and Forbes had agreed to use Bailey as a plant: convince her the wicked city was no place for someone like her. By the time he was finished, Miss Dairy Farm would hightail it back to the land of milk and cheese and thank him for it.

He peered out the russet-colored miniblinds of her room to the parking lot. A number of cars were parked in front, but at 3:00 a.m., the streets and the area outside the sleazy motel were fairly deserted.

Sounds filtered through the thin walls of adjacent rooms. A shoot-out from an old western movie competed with the squeak of rusty bedsprings and raucous laughter.

Working vice, he'd been in any number of run-down establishments throughout the city of Los Angeles, but this place at least attempted to give the appearance of clean, even if it did rent rooms by the hour.

"Hurry it up," he called to Bailey.

The bathroom door opened and steam billowed into the room. Bailey followed. "Let me get my things," she said, unwrapping a thin towel from her hair and shaking the long, damp strands loose.

Mason stared. After all his years on the force, not many things shocked or surprised him, but the sight of Bailey, the *real* Bailey without lady-of-the-evening apparel or heavy cosmetics that hid delicate features, nearly blew his mind. She wore a pair of well-worn jeans that hugged gently rounded hips and showed off legs that erotic dreams were made of. A butter-yellow cotton T-shirt tucked into the denim outlined breasts needing no enhancement. She was petite and stunningly beautiful. She was peaches-and-cream, softness and woman all the way through, from the top of her golden head all the way down to her glossy pink, painted toenails. She was the girl next door, and the last woman on earth he wanted to be responsible for protecting.

She bent and plucked a canvas gym bag from the floor to set on the dresser, then leaned over to retrieve items from the bottom drawer. She pulled out a handful of lacy, whisper-soft panties, and his mouth went dry just imagining them covering her secrets.

"Where are we going?" she asked, stuffing lingerie into the gym bag, oblivious to the steamy fantasy playing through his mind.

"A safe house," he said sharply, too sharply, since she glanced over her shoulder at him, a light frown marring her forehead. There was going to be nothing safe about living under the same roof with her for the next few days. Not if he used his physical reaction to her as a barometer.

She closed the drawer then opened another. This one held a pair of white shorts, another pair of jeans and a few tops. She dropped them into the bag on top of the lacy things. "I'd like to phone my mother and let her know where I can be reached, in case she hears from my sister."

"She can leave a message for you at the department," he said, and started pacing the room. He'd like nothing more than to take her to the nearest Greyhound station and send her packing back to Wisconsin. To a place where she'd be safe, not only from the danger she was more than willing to face, but from him and the carnal turn his thoughts had taken. "No one is to know where you're staying."

She opened her mouth to say something, then snapped it closed and continued packing. He saw the red siren's dress go into the bag, followed by a prim white nightgown. Five minutes later she sat on the edge of the bed to pull on thick white socks and a pair of sneakers. She tied the laces into bows then looked up at him, purpose evident in her gaze.

She stood. "You don't want to do this, do you?"

He stopped pacing and swung around to face

her. "You're damn right I don't." He thought of Ashley Adams. He thought of innocence stolen and a young life ended too soon. She couldn't have been much older than Bailey. "You don't know what can go wrong. I do."

"Then why don't you tell me," she suggested, her calm, serene voice a direct contrast to the determination glowing in her eyes. Determination that could end her life.

"You could get killed," he replied with blunt honesty.

Her pink lips twitched with something akin to a half smile. "You'll protect me, O'Neill."

He closed the distance between them to glare down at her. "You don't know squat about me."

"I know enough to know you helped me last night when that kid tried to make me go with him."

He didn't say anything, just frowned at her.

"And you stopped me from approaching Shore tonight," she continued. "Are you trying to say those are the acts of a man who won't do whatever is necessary to keep me alive?"

He blew out a stream of breath in frustration. "You're taking an awful lot for granted. People make mistakes. Judgment is skewed by emotion, namely fear. There are unexpected variables in every scenario. Too many of those variables and people die."

She shrugged and stepped around him. "Then it's a chance I'll have to take," she said, hoisting the gym bag over her shoulder. "Because I'm not leaving, O'Neill."

Mason bit back a curse. He wanted to scare her off, to make her see the reality of the situation for what it was—she could end up dead, and then who would "save" her sister? Instead, she was practically laughing at him.

She slung the bag she used for a purse over her other shoulder and headed toward the door. "I know what you're up to, O'Neill. It won't work. I'm not leaving L.A. without my sister."

Mason watched her saunter out the door bold as you please. She stepped up to the Bronco and waited for him to unlock the door. With a muttered curse, he followed, his gut telling him he was making one whopper of a mistake.

And there wasn't a damn thing he could do about it except ride it out.

4

UNABLE TO SLEEP, Bailey slipped from under the sheets and silently padded to the window overlooking the predawn Los Angeles skyline. Cool air from the air-conditioning brushed against her skin, and she shivered. Rubbing her hands over her arms to generate warmth, she propped her shoulder against the stucco wall to wait for the sun to break over the horizon.

The adrenaline rush she'd been running on for most of the night had faded by the time they'd arrived at the safe house, and she'd barely been able to keep her eyes open long enough to strip off her jeans and crawl into the huge four-poster bed. With less than three hours' sleep, her eyes felt grainy and her body lethargic, but her mind refused to shut down. *How could it?* she thought, turning from the window. After the scare she'd had thinking the poor girl they'd found could have been Leslie, she didn't think she'd sleep peacefully again until her sister was safely beside her. After her previous experience with the cops, she was reluctant to admit she finally had her first real ray of hope in finding her sister.

Knowing sleep was impossible, she dug through her bag and retrieved her robe. The last thing she wanted was to run into O'Neill wearing nothing but a T-shirt and a smile.

She slipped into the white terry cloth and looped the belt before quietly stepping into the hallway. She waited for her eyes to adjust to the darkness and listened for a sign that O'Neill was awake, but the only sound came from the gentle hum of the central air-conditioning unit. Recalling her steps through the house only hours ago, the spacious living room was straight ahead. And hopefully the kitchen and much-needed, and rejuvenating, coffee.

Keeping close to the wall, she used her hands to guide her, stepping carefully since she couldn't remember if there had been anything to impede her progress. Something soft and silky brushed against her hand. She jumped back, a tight squeal of fear lodging in her throat before she recalled the tall, oblong table with a silk flower arrangement. Willing her heart rate to return to normal, she stepped around the table and continued toward the front of the house.

She reached the open area of the living room and stopped. The drapes had been left open, allowing the pale, predawn light to aid her in gaining her bearings. In the semidarkness, she made out the shapes of furniture and spotted a lamp across the room. She turned, and saw the shadow of a man looming in front of her.

A scream lodged in her throat when he reached for her. Her feet tangled in her robe, and she fell to the floor, taking the man with her. Pain shot from her hip, momentarily overshadowing her fear.

Finding her voice, she cried out, hoping to rouse O'Neill, and struggled against her attacker.

She tried to push him off her, but he was as unmovable as a mountain. A large hand clamped over her lips when she opened her mouth to scream, so she bit down into the callused flesh.

Her attacker swore a blue streak.

"Dammit, Bailey."

Relief washed over her at the sound of O'Neill's rough, angry voice, and she sagged against the cold stone tiles.

"What are you doing sneaking around in the middle of the night?" he demanded.

"I wasn't sneaking around," she told him, her eyes adjusting to the dimness of the room. The robe she'd thought would provide modesty lay open, making her very conscious of his thick, muscled, denim-covered thighs pressed against her bare ones. "I didn't want to wake you."

She peered up at him, and expected an angry glare in return. Instead, he watched her with an intensity that unnerved her. His face was inches from hers, his warm breath fanning her cheek. If she turned her head slightly, only a heartbeat would separate their lips. All she had to do was...

His gaze slid down the length of her, encouraging her runaway fantasy. "What did you want?"

She stared at those lips only inches from hers. *He has such a nice mouth,* she thought. "Coffee."

He eased himself off her and settled back on his haunches. "Are you all right?" he asked gently.

"I think so. Just bruised," she said, telling herself her skyrocketing pulse rate had nothing to do with the sudden husky, loverlike softness of his voice, but with the fright he'd given her. She eased up on her elbows, tearing her gaze away from those lips that had her curious about deep kisses and one surly detective.

A frown drew his dark eyebrows together. "Where?"

She blinked, trying to focus on the conversation and not on the idea that she'd actually considered kissing O'Neill. "My hip."

He pushed her robe farther aside. "Let me see," he said when she tried to tug the terry cloth around her.

She sat up and winced. "I'm fine."

He gave her a look that said he didn't believe her and ran his hand up her thigh and over her hip. His palm was rough and hot. Or was it just that her skin heated beneath his touch? She didn't know for certain, but the thought went right out of her mind when his hand skimmed the lace edge of her panties. Her breath caught, and an odd stirring started in her tummy and wove through her.

"Does that hurt?" he asked as if he hadn't just tilted her world. He gently pressed his fingers against her skin, skin that suddenly felt too tight for her body.

"I said I was fine." She scooted away and stood, pulling her robe around her traitorous body. "Do you always tackle your guests first thing in the morning?"

He stood and looked down at her. His expression turned to granite. "You're not a guest. You're under my protection since you don't have the brains to stay out of trouble and let the police handle this situation."

Now *that* was the O'Neill she understood. The cranky one. And she would do well to remember that in the future and forget about kisses and tender touches and resulting tummy flutters. "Can we argue later? After coffee, perhaps?"

O'Neill grunted a reply, then brushed past her, muttering something she couldn't quite make out, but was certain was yards away from flattering. She followed him and rubbed her sore hip.

He flipped a switch on the wall and the hum of fluorescent lighting filled the kitchen, revealing a unique combination of high-tech and rustic charm. She pulled out a stool at the tiled breakfast bar and sat while O'Neill filled the carafe with water.

"Do the taxpayers know about this place?" She wasn't certain what she expected of a safe house, but it certainly wasn't a sprawling Spanish-style ranch home nestled high in the Hollywood Hills complete with courtyard and ivy-covered fountain behind a coded security gate.

Mason filled the basket with coffee grounds and kept his back to Bailey. She was rumpled and sexy, and he didn't think he'd ever forget the satiny feel of her skin beneath his hands, or the way her lace panties hid nothing and everything. Reminding himself they would be living under the same roof for a few days because of the job did nothing to alleviate his inappropriate thoughts.

"If they did," he said, turning on the coffee-maker, "we wouldn't be calling it a safe house, now, would we?"

He turned in time to see her shrug. She propped her elbows on the bar and rested her chin in her hands. Dark shadows underscored her eyes, reminding him they'd both had little sleep. He should order her back to bed. He needed her alert and watchful if they were going to pull off the sting and nail Shore. He'd told her there were variables, that mistakes happen and people die, but she'd chosen to ignore his warnings. Since he didn't have a choice, he planned to make it his personal mission to abate as many variables as possible to keep Bailey safe. If they were damn lucky, maybe they'd even find her sister alive. Only, too many years on the force made him doubt the possibility.

The coffeemaker stopped gurgling, and he poured them each a mug before pulling out the stool across from her. Setting his coffee on the bar, he opened a drawer then snapped a yellow notepad and pen down in front of him. "Why did your sister run away from home?"

She wrapped her slender fingers around the mug and lifted it to her lips. "You don't believe in beating around the bush, do you, O'Neill?" she asked after taking a sip of coffee.

"Every minute your sister is with Shore, she's in danger," he told her bluntly. He could tell her his doubts about finding Leslie Grayson alive, but chose to keep those suspicions to himself. Whether or not his decision was based on not wanting to upset Bailey, or thinking that she'd be useful in nailing Shore, he couldn't say, and that irritated him. He didn't want to believe he was becoming so desperate to bring Shore down that he'd sacrifice an innocent woman—again.

"Do you want to waste time with couched phrases and sugarcoated words?" he asked, shoving the past firmly where it belonged—in the past.

She sighed and set her mug on the counter. "No." She pushed a long strand of hair behind her ear. "No, I guess I don't."

He picked up the pen and gave her a pointed look. "Why did your sister run away from home?" he asked again. He'd been a cop long enough to know that too many runaways chose the streets to avoid bad situations at home. And he'd busted enough of them to know that some form of abuse was generally the leading reason for their escape.

"My father died of a heart attack about a year and a half ago. Six months ago, my mother remarried."

He made a few notes on the pad. "Problems with the stepfather," he muttered, more to himself than her.

She tilted her head to the side and looked at him with those big blue eyes. "Problems?"

"Yeah, like an 'unnatural' interest in your sister."

She shook her head vehemently. "No. Les was really close to our dad, and she's had a hard time adjusting. When my mom remarried, Les felt like Mom replaced him."

Bailey bristled at O'Neill's skeptical expression. Ned would never do anything to hurt Leslie, or her mother. Of that she was certain. Leslie ran away for another reason entirely, and it was her fault.

Guilt swamped her. She slid off the bar stool and strode to the window overlooking a copse of evergreen trees. Shoving her hands in the pockets of her robe, she watched a group of sparrows flit from one branch to the next. The truth was, Leslie had felt alone, with no one to turn to, and Bailey blamed herself.

"Are you sure?" O'Neill asked softly.

"I've known Ned Tuttle my entire life," she answered quietly, keeping her back to him. "I'm positive."

"So why'd she run away?" he repeated.

She turned to face him. However reluctantly, he'd offered to help her, and he deserved to know the truth. "I let her down." There, she'd said it. She'd openly admitted her guilt, and the ground didn't open up to swallow her.

His eyebrows pulled into a frown. "You?"

She nodded. "I wasn't there for her. When my dad died, I should have moved back home, but I didn't. I stayed in Milwaukee." And concentrated on her career. The truth was, returning to the farm had been the last thing on earth she'd ever wanted to do. She had happy memories from her childhood, but she'd been no different from any other small-town kid anxious to escape to the big city and bright lights, and make her mark on the world.

Her family hadn't been poor by any means, but there had rarely been money left over each month for anything other than necessities. Repairs on equipment, the purchase of winter feed for livestock, or a roof in need of mending took the place of family vacations or new vehicles. In Milwaukee, for the first time in her life she had money that was hers. She hadn't wanted to relinquish the freedom she'd gained by moving away from home. Instead of returning to Whitewater when her father died, she'd selfishly remained in Milwaukee with her foot on the bottom rung of the corporate ladder.

He set the pen on the counter and reached for his coffee. "You can't take the blame because your sister—"

"I've always taken care of her," she cut him off. She'd told herself the same thing hundreds of times in the weeks since Leslie's disappearance. She'd even dipped into her savings and hired an investigator. But nothing eliminated the truth, or her guilt; she'd shirked her responsibility and failed her family.

She moved away from the window and returned to the bar stool. "I'm the oldest by seven years, and it's been my responsibility for as long as I can remember to look after my little sister. My parents were busy. They had a dairy farm to run and a family to support. The hours are long and the work is hard. Whenever Leslie needed anything, I was the one to see to it that it was taken care of. She needed me and I wasn't there for her."

His eyes filled with a warmth and compassion that had her thinking he wasn't always such a grump. "You can't blame yourself," he repeated reasonably. "You have your own life to lead."

She reached for her coffee and took a sip. "Where I come from, family is always first," she argued. She set her mug back on the tiled breakfast bar and trailed her finger along the grouted squares. "I chose to build my career, instead. I let my sister down, and my family, when they really needed me. I'm going to make it up to them and bring Leslie home."

He reached across the bar and covered her hand with his, his gentle touch filling her with warmth. "I know about disappointing the people you love."

The phone on the far wall rang, and O'Neill withdrew his hand and strode across the kitchen. He picked up the receiver. "Yeah?"

She sipped her coffee and kept her gaze on O'Neill's broad shoulders. He wore the same loose-fitting shirt and faded jeans he'd worn earlier, but his shoulder holster was missing. Missing, but not far away, she realized as she spotted the lethal weapon on the counter within easy reach.

"I'll find out," O'Neill said into the phone. He looked at her, his eyebrows drawn together. The compassion she'd suspected earlier had faded, and he was all cop again. She could see it in his defensive stance and hear it in the sudden hardness of his voice. "You're sure?"

She stood and headed toward the coffeepot for more blessed caffeine. Her tummy grumbled, and she wondered how difficult a search she'd have in locating a loaf of bread to make some toast.

"Just the usual," he said after a few moments. "And tell Hammond to bring my dog. I don't know how long we'll be here, and Jo can't be left alone for too long."

By the time he hung up the phone, she had two slices of bread browning in the toaster oven. Whoever's job it was to make sure the safe house was well stocked deserved a raise, she thought, pulling a jar of her favorite brand of raspberry preserves from the refrigerator.

"Tell me about the investigator you hired," O'Neill demanded in what she was learning was his "cop voice."

She pulled the toast from the toaster oven, trying to ignore the sense of dread filling her. "William

Greene?" she asked cautiously, spreading a thin layer of margarine on the toast.

She glanced over her shoulder at him. He closed his eyes briefly and rubbed the back of his neck. "Yeah," he said, looking at her. "William Greene. When was the last time you heard from him?"

Turning her attention back to the toast, she methodically added a small dollop of jam. She wasn't going to like what he had to say; she could see it in his eyes. *Please, no,* she thought, carefully setting the toast on a paper towel.

"Two weeks ago," she said, turning to face him, "when he told me that he'd heard Leslie had been seen with Devlin Shore. He said he was going to obtain confirmation, but I never heard from him again."

"He's dead, Bailey," he said bluntly.

She gripped the counter behind her for support. "How do you know it's him?" she asked, hating that her voice sounded so far away.

Her legs buckled but O'Neill was in front of her in an instant, his hands gripping her shoulders to keep her from sliding to the floor.

"There was ID on the body," he said. "There's no doubt it's Greene. I'm sorry, Bailey."

She looked up at him, at that compassion glowing in his warm, honey-colored eyes, and felt the first sting of moisture burn her gaze. "Why?" she asked on a choked cry.

"My guess is he got too close."

"Mason, I have to find my sister. God, what if she's already..." She couldn't finish the thought, couldn't vocalize her greatest fear. She knew Devlin Shore was a criminal. The information she'd learned about him on the streets and from William Greene indicated his criminal activities stretched far beyond the peddling of flesh. Nevertheless, in her innocence, she'd never dreamed that murder would be a part of Shore's notorious résumé. Nor, that by hiring Greene, she'd send the man to his death.

Mason pulled her into the circle of his strong arms, and held her against his wide chest. "Don't, Bailey," he said soothingly, gently running his hand along her spine. "Don't blame yourself. You can't keep torturing yourself like this."

She slipped her arms around his middle and held on tight, needing to be held, needing and accepting the physical comfort he offered. The sound of his heart beat rhythmically against her cheek. Steady. Sure.

She pulled back and looked up at him. "Help me, Mason," she pleaded. "Promise me you'll help find my sister."

Gently, he lifted his hand and trailed his knuckles along her cheek. "I will. I promise."

He cupped her cheek in his palm and she turned toward the warmth generated by his hand. His eyes darkened, the warm honeyed glow turning a deep tawny color. The fluttering started in her tummy again, and a heaviness settled between her thighs. He was going to kiss her. She wasn't sure how or why she knew, but she did. She wanted to feel his lips pressed against hers and briefly forget the ugliness.

Just as she suspected, O'Neill lowered his head and brushed his lips softly against hers. A jolt the equivalent of an electrical charge surged through her at that first tentative touch of lips. She'd been kissed before, yet she'd never experienced such a rush of energy. The one thing she hadn't shed along with her small-town image was her virginity. Some lessons in life were hard-pressed to fall by the wayside, and her mother's constant lectures on "good girls don't" were seeded deeply inside her. Besides, there was something incredibly romantic about waiting for the right man to come along, about knowing the moment he touched you that he was the one you'd been waiting for all your life.

At least that's what she'd told herself when her twenty-fourth birthday had rolled around a few months ago.

He moved slowly, as if he understood her inexperience. The hand against her cheek slid into her hair to cup the back of her neck. He deepened the kiss, his tongue gently sweeping inside, coaxing her until she tentatively tangled her tongue with his. When he groaned against her mouth, the fluttering in her tummy tightened, making her feel restless inside.

He pulled her closer. Her breasts pressed against his chest and her nipples tightened. Heat pooled in her belly and wove through her. Even someone with her inexperience could name the physical demands of her body. Desire. Desire and need for O'Neill.

She splayed her hands over his back, testing the feel of the taut, well-muscled flesh beneath her fingertips. The man was a startling combination of power and gentleness, and he awakened something inside her she'd never experienced. Something she feared went deeper than desire, further than need, and was more complicated than sex. Something more emotional she didn't yet understand, and was unsure she wanted to explore.

He pulled away suddenly, and the clouds of passion slowly parted. She sucked in a deep breath, hoping her legs would support her. Was she really trembling? She shoved her hands into the pockets of her robe, praying he wouldn't notice how badly they shook.

He scrubbed his hand down his face. "We can't do this," he said, his voice sounding tight and strained.

A buzzer sounded, indicating someone was at the security gate demanding entrance. O'Neill brushed past her, snagged his pistol off the counter and left her standing alone in the kitchen.

Part of her was grateful he'd ended the kiss.

Another part of her, the most basic, she realized, wanted him to carry her into one of the many bedrooms of the safe house and make love to her.

5

MASON MADE a sound of disgust, then wrapped his fingers around Bailey's slender forearm before she clipped him a second time. She'd walloped him a good one, but her form was wrong and she could've broken her wrist. Bailey was his responsibility and he wanted her ready—for anything. If Ashley had been prepared, she might be alive today.

"Like this," he told Bailey, fighting to hold on to his patience while pressing her palm open with his free hand. Slowly, he brought her hand to his jaw, showing her the proper angle and technique again.

To her credit, she hadn't whined once about the grueling pace he'd kept her under for the past three hours, or argued with him about the basic self-defense techniques he was teaching her in an attempt to arm her. He'd quickly dismissed Blake's suggestion of providing her with a weapon. If their plan worked and Bailey did manage to lure Shore, chances were that he'd have her searched. Arming her wasn't a risk he wanted to take.

"Right here," he ordered sternly, repeating the motion. "Keep your palm open. The bones at the base of a woman's hand are the strongest in her body. Use them to your advantage."

Instead of complaining, she nodded, then took a

deep breath when he released her arm. He knew she was beat. And he suspected she realized he was close to the end of his patience.

"Maybe you should knock off for a while." Blake appeared in the doorway, his hands thrust in the pockets of his neatly creased trousers. Upon his arrival, he'd informed them that the female undercover officer Lieutenant Forbes had planned to send was off duty and couldn't be located. That left the two of them to prepare Bailey. Mason was not happy.

"Not until she has this right," he said, giving his partner a hard look. "Do you think Shore'll give her a break?"

Blake knew the risks as well as he did, and Mason didn't have to remind his partner that sometime in the next thirty-six hours, Bailey's life would probably be on the line. There would be no breaks until he was satisfied with her progress.

"Why do I need to know all this?" she asked, practicing the movements he'd taught her. "You're going to be there, right?"

Standing by her side while she attempted to lure Shore was out of the question. She'd be under surveillance, and although he was determined not to let her out of his sight, he still wanted her prepared. If she found herself alone with the man, or worse, in danger, she needed to be able to incapacitate him, if even for the few moments necessary to attempt an escape or give the cops time to move in and do their job.

"Variables," he said, shaking his head when her hand missed the mark again. He guided her hand toward his jaw, and held it there. His fingers itched to caress her velvet-soft skin. Her fingers flexed against his cheek, causing awareness to rumble through him. "Variables can end your life. A few seconds can also save it."

"We should go over the plan with her," Blake reminded him, bending down to pat Jo on the side.

The German shepherd's bushy tail thumped in appreciation against the thick mat, but she kept her attention on Mason. He didn't have the heart to put the retired canine in a kennel for however long he'd be with Bailey in the safe house, so he'd had Blake pick her up from his place. For the past two years Jo had been his constant companion, ever since the department retired her at the age of seven. Jo was getting old, but nowhere near over-the-hill as far as he was concerned.

Blake straightened, then resumed his casual stance against the doorjamb. "I want to fit her with the wire. She needs to get used to wearing it."

Mason frowned. "Later," he said. "And *I'll* fit her with the wire, Hammond."

Blake lifted an eyebrow, no doubt questioning his territorial response, and grinned. When Mason glared, Blake simply shrugged and left them alone in the gym at the back of the house.

There was no way Mason was going to allow his womanizing partner that close to Bailey. Maybe it had something to do with the kiss they'd shared earlier. Or maybe it was her scent, or the way her body molded so perfectly against his. Or even the fact that she'd trembled in his arms when he'd held her.

Sweet heaven, he couldn't remember the last time a woman actually trembled in his arms, and from something as simple as a kiss. But there'd been nothing simple about that kiss. There'd been need and desire and longing. A longing so fierce, he could still feel it pulsating through his body.

"All right, let's try this again," Mason said, dragging his thoughts away from tasting Bailey's lips, lips that had stirred more than his libido. Even the plain lavender top tucked into white shorts stirred his imagination.

As he'd taught her, she opened her hand, fingers back, and slowly brought the base of her palm toward his jaw.

"Better," he said. "If someone grabs your arm, I want this to be second nature to you. Understand?"

"I got it, O'Neill."

"You go for the jaw. It'll stun them. You go for the nose, straight up and with as much power as you can manage, you'll render them unconscious, or even kill them by driving the cartilage into the brain if you use enough force."

She made a face, clearly indicating her view on that subject. He wasn't about to mollycoddle her. She wanted to play undercover cop, then she'd damn well be able to defend herself until he could reach her if things got sticky. "It's you or the bad guy, Bailey. Remember that. Only one person wins, and it'd better be you."

She sighed in exasperation. "I got it, O'Neill," she said again, her tone indicating she was tiring of his lectures.

"Just don't forget it," he added, turning away.

Abruptly, before she could think, he swung back around, roughly grabbing her upper arm. She looked stunned for all of two seconds. Using what little weight she had, she pivoted and solidly connected the base of her palm with his jaw. His ears rang, causing him to take a step back and release her.

She stared at him for a moment, her mouth gaping. "It worked!" Her face filled with wonder and awe as she looked from him to her hand and back again. "It really worked," she said, her lips curving into a blinding smile.

He moved his jaw. "It's supposed to," he complained, then rubbed at the spot where she'd connected. For such a little thing, she had enough upper-body strength to at least manage to break free should such tactics become necessary to her survival.

"Ohmigosh," she said, coming toward him. A worried frown creased her forehead as she reached up and gingerly pressed her fingers against his skin. Her scent, sweet and intoxicating, wrapped around him, making him want to yank away the clip holding back her hair so he could bury his hands in the soft tresses, draw her close and taste her lips once again.

"Are you okay?" she asked. "I'm so sorry, Mason."

Her touch, her scent, hell, even being in the same room with her distracted him. They could ill afford distractions. "I'm fine," he said, pulling away. "One more technique, then we'll take a break for a while."

She sighed, but kept the complaint he sensed hovering on her lips to herself.

He stepped in front of her, torturing himself by bringing their bodies close together. "Hold my arms," he commanded, and waited until she placed her hands over his biceps, her grip firm but gentle.

"Watch closely." He brought his hands between them and gently pushed outward, forcing her to let go of him. "Next," he said, "knee him in the groin as hard as you can. That'll bring your assailant down, toward you. When he falls forward, you go up with your hands. Like this." As if scooping cool water with his hands, he brought them up and gently pressed the tips of his fingers against Bailey's delicate throat.

"Do it right, with a short jab, you immobilize him. Wrong, you've just busted your fingers."

She propped her hands on her slender hips, drawing his attention to her tanned, lithe legs. "Why can't I just do the fingers-in-the-throat thing?"

"Because you won't have any mobility. You're too short. You'll never reach if someone's holding you." To demonstrate, he held her arms just above the elbow. "Try it."

She did, and quickly realized he was right. She blew out a frustrated stream of breath that ruffled her bangs. For the next twenty minutes, she practiced it his way, and failed.

Mason shoved his hands through his hair. "Dammit, Bailey. Concentrate."

"I am." Her eyes filled with fire, matching the heat in her voice.

He spun her around and grasped her hips, pulling her tight against him. "Feel my body. Move with it," he said. Her bottom nestled against him was pure torture. Heat shot to his groin like a rocket. "Put your hands on my arms," he snapped.

She did, further aligning her body with his. Sweet heaven, how much was a man supposed to take? He raised his forearms and pushed outward. Using his knee, he forced hers up, then followed through with the jab to the imaginary assailant's throat.

Bailey moved to step away, to gain some valuable distance from the man making her heart race and her blood pound in her ears, but he pulled her tighter against him. A few minutes of torture, of having his hard, lean body pressed intimately against hers, was a small price to pay when it could save her sister's life, she told herself.

"Again," he ordered, and repeated the moves he was attempting to teach her.

Using the mirrored walls of the gym, she kept her gaze on his, allowing her body to follow his movements, feeling every hard line of him pressed into her. He smelled of musk and man, and she resisted the urge to turn in his arms and request a repeat performance of the kiss they'd shared earlier that morning. The only thing that kept her from following through on that little fantasy was the determination in his eyes.

Determination, and something else she didn't recognize.

"Second nature, Bailey. You've got to be able to do this in your sleep." His deep voice rumbled against her back, causing her insides to flutter.

The only thing that was becoming second nature was the way her heart raced every time the denim of his jeans rubbed against her bare legs. Or the way her heart pounded when his firm, wide chest pressed into her, or when he lowered his head and his warm breath brushed her cheek as he offered encouragement. Not exactly the stuff romantic dreams were made of, she thought, but was affected nonetheless.

She moved. He held her against him. She couldn't take much more. Her insides had gone from fluttering to churning with anticipation and what she was beginning to recognize as need. She dropped her gaze to where his hand held her hip. Did his fingers really flex against her, or was her imagination working overtime? She lifted her eyes and met his in the mirror. The determination she'd detected earlier shifted, and something else flared to life. Something hot and demanding, something that said the sensations coursing through her body were equaled in his. Something that said he wanted her as much as she wanted him.

Dear Lord, what was happening to her? She'd never lusted after a man before. Never felt the wild and insistent demands of need or desire to the extent that O'Neill aroused within her. She hardly knew him, yet her body responded to him in a way that should have frightened her, but excited her, instead.

His hand slipped from her hip and skirted the edge of her shorts, brushing teasingly along her thigh. Thoughts of "good girls don't" flew right out of her head.

"O'Neill?" she questioned, her voice barely above a whisper.

He responded by dipping his head and nuzzling her neck. She sighed as a shiver chased down her spine, igniting a spark deep inside her. His hands moved up and down her sides, his fingers lightly brushing against the sides of her breasts, then skimming her hips to pull her tighter against him. Her nipples beaded and rubbed against the lacy cups of her bra, the sensation as erotic as if they'd been cradled in his palms.

She wanted to touch him, to make him feel as wonderfully sensuous as he made her feel. To see for herself if his skin felt as tight as hers, or if he suffered the same restlessness caused by the hot brand of a touch.

His tongue outlined the shell of her ear, sending a delightfully wicked sensation through her body. She watched in the mirror as his hands left her hips to travel over her tummy and upward to cup her breasts. Unable to watch their erotic images any longer, she closed her eyes and rested her head against his chest. When he cupped her breasts in his hands, she arched against him. Good Lord, she was on fire.

Frustrated at not being able to touch him, she shifted, turning to wreathe her arms around his neck. "Kiss me, O'Neill," she demanded, pulling his mouth toward hers.

Mason complied, and tasted heaven. But he needed his head examined. They were playing with fire.

He reveled in the flames licking through him at her sweet and gentle touch.

He'd never been one to make foolish choices. Methodical and detailed were more his speed. Carefully examine the situation, then act accordingly. The skills he'd honed over the years, the ones that had kept him alive in difficult circumstances, fled when Bailey moaned against his mouth. He was headed for trouble and knew it. And he chose to ignore the warning signs, instead striking a path on the road that led him straight into the danger zone.

Plain, old-fashioned lust ruled him. Admitting his attraction to her was one thing, but it was quite another to allow his body to overrule his common sense. And where Bailey Grayson was concerned, sense, common or otherwise, became nonexistent the minute her cornflower eyes filled with heat, desire and need.

Instead of setting her away from him, he pulled her closer and ran his hands down her back to cup her bottom. She arched into him, and he hardened in a flash. She tasted sweet and as hot as the bright California sunshine.

She tugged his T-shirt out of the waistband of his jeans. His control slipped several notches when she smoothed her hands over his back and along his rib cage. After their kiss this morning, he'd been so sure he could put her out of his mind. He'd convinced himself that that kiss had been a fluke: a simple gesture of comfort that had been taken a little too far. Now, that confidence fled. It wasn't as if he was concerned about a relationship with Bailey. He wasn't in the market for anything long-term. Relationships and cops didn't mix, and he had the divorce decree to prove it.

He knew enough about women to know that the one moaning against his mouth and running her hands over his body in exploration would never settle for a no-strings affair. She was the picket-fence type, the traditional, forever, set-of-matching-gold-bands kind of woman. And that meant hands off for a guy like him.

He tore his mouth from her insistent lips and set her away from him. They had a job to do. Once that job was over and Shore was behind bars where he belonged, he and Bailey would go their separate ways. End of discussion…until she looked at him with those wide blue eyes filled with confusion and need.

His hands traveled from her shoulders to her face. "Bailey—"

"Maybe we *should* take a break," she said abruptly.

She stepped out of his reach and turned away, but not before he saw the wounded expression in her eyes. God, he felt as if he'd just kicked a litter of puppies.

She ran her hands over her hips as if wiping sweat from her palms. "I've had enough, O'Neill. I'm tired."

He nodded, not trusting himself to tell her the truth, that he wanted nothing more than to make love to her. He watched her go, back straight and head held high, convinced he'd done right by stopping before things got too far out of control. He was saving them both from making one horrendous mistake.

He dropped onto the weight bench. Jo trotted across the room and laid her head on his knee, her dark almond-shaped eyes looking up at him expectantly. "You don't believe it, either, do you, old girl," he said, scratching Jo behind the ears. The dog's tail wagged, and she nudged his leg with her muzzle.

He stood, and left the room, Jo running by his side. As he made his way down the long corridor toward the bedrooms, he heard the sound of water running, indicating Bailey had decided to take a shower. Imagining the water sluicing over her petite and curvy body did nothing to alleviate his already overheated response to her. He stopped by her door, wondering what would happen if he slipped into her room and joined her. Would she order him out? Or would she show him the slice of heaven he imagined he'd find in her arms?

Heaven, he decided, and strode past her door.

6

BAILEY CROSSED her arms over her chest and glared at O'Neill. "You're not being fair," she said angrily. "You have no idea how I'll *react*."

O'Neill braced his hands on the smoked-glass dining table and leaned forward, his expression thunderous. "You're too green. You're going to get yourself killed."

She'd been arguing with him for the past ten minutes, fighting to convince him she would not panic when faced with a dangerous, and potentially deadly, situation, and was getting nowhere fast. Somewhere between leaving the warmth of his arms and stepping from a cold shower that did nothing to diminish her aroused state, O'Neill had changed his mind again and was prepared to browbeat her into leaving. He'd just have to get over it, she thought. She wasn't leaving. Not until she had her sister.

"Ms. Grayson. Bailey," Blake interrupted, giving O'Neill a look filled with exasperation. "What my partner is trying to say is that Devlin Shore is a very dangerous man. We suspect he's responsible for the death of the investigator you hired."

Bailey turned her attention to Blake, relieved to find understanding in his smokey gaze. "I realize you think that, but how do you know for certain?

Los Angeles is a big city. He could've been mugged or something."

O'Neill shoved away from the table and straightened. "Shore left his calling card. He has a particular style, one that we're not unfamiliar with. Trust me, Bailey. He took care of Greene personally."

Her gaze flicked from Blake to O'Neill. She knew O'Neill was trying to frighten her away, and suspected this was just another one of his transparent tactics. "How can you be sure?"

He crossed the small dining area off the kitchen to pull out a bar stool. "Greene obviously got too close," he said, propping his backside on the stool. He leaned back, his elbows braced on the ceramic-tile counter. "We've seen it before. Let us do our jobs, Bailey. Go home."

She leveled her gaze on him. "We've already had this discussion. I'm not leaving." Turning her attention back to Blake, she asked, "How long have you been after Shore?"

"Long enough," O'Neill answered for him.

She struggled to ignore him, which was no easy chore considering how she'd clung to him little more than an hour ago. The man affected her, but she was coming to terms with that little truth. A heated look had the power to make her knees weak. A touch could make her quiver with need. And a kiss had her thinking "good girls don't" was an antiquated expression and tangled sheets and damp bodies was the way to go.

She kept her attention on Blake. "How long, Detective Hammond?"

He set the documents he'd been holding on the table and looked at her. He had nice eyes, she thought, filled with intelligence and compassion. She imagined that his deep, velvet-soft voice combined with the aura of concern he presented came in handy in police work. She hid a smile. She could easily envision Blake Hammond and O'Neill playing good cop, bad cop. And guess who got to play bad cop?

"Four years," Blake said.

She leaned forward and folded her arms on the glass tabletop. "And he always manages to elude you," she stated. She heard O'Neill make a noise close to a sound of disgust and continued to ignore him. She didn't have to see his face to know he was scowling again. "You said last night you need someone on the inside. I can do this, Detective Hammond."

"Do you want to end up like Greene," O'Neill demanded, coming off the bar stool, "with a bullet lodged in your skull?" He shoved his hand through his hair and gave her a hard look. His eyes held none of the compassion she sensed in his partner.

"If you're found out... If all Shore does is kill you," O'Neill said, "you'll consider yourself lucky."

Horrifying images filtered through her mind, and she suppressed a shudder of revulsion. There was no way she was going to give O'Neill an inkling of how truly frightened the thought of facing down Devlin Shore made her. She feared if he so much as suspected she was terrified, he'd find a way to keep her from going through with the plan. As long as her sister's life was on the line, she'd never give up.

"Can we go over the plan now, Detective Hammond?" she asked. His full mouth crooked into a slight grin filled with compassion. All she had to do was concentrate on finding Leslie. Nothing else mattered.

She stood and headed into the kitchen for a glass of water, needing something to wash away the revulsion clogging her throat. *Think of Leslie,* she told herself silently, taking a glass from the cupboard. *Just think of her, and you can do anything.*

She filled the glass with cool tap water, and turned around to find O'Neill towering above her. He took the glass from her and set it on the counter. His hands settled on her shoulders as he waited for her to look up at him. When she did, the hardness was still there, mingled with concern.

"Listen to me, Bailey," he said, his deep voice filled with conviction. "Shore isn't just a pimp. He's involved in a hell of a lot more. Guns. Drugs. Murder. Those are just a few of his more recent activities."

She moved to step away from him.

He tightened his grip.

"His lucky victims end up with a bullet to the back of their skull," he said bluntly. "The more unfortunate ones require dental records for identification."

She struggled to keep her expression blank. *Think of Leslie. Nothing will keep you from finding her. Nothing!*

She shrugged out of his grasp, surprised when he let her go. "Then that's all the more reason for me to find my sister. I know what I'm doing, O'Neill."

"The hell you do," he roared. He pulled in a deep breath, and she sensed his war with control. Control was important to him, she realized suddenly, and her curiosity climbed a notch. She'd sensed that iron will of his when they were in the gym together. That same will, she suspected, that he'd summoned to end their passion before they went beyond caresses and kisses.

"Dammit, Bailey," he said, his voice a harsh whisper. "Why are you so intent on putting your life at risk?"

She wanted to reach out to him. To lay her hand gently against his cheek and attempt to ease his mind. She kept her hands to herself, instead. "Maybe for the same reason you do it every day of your life," she answered.

She stepped around him, and he didn't stop her. Returning to the table, she sat. "I'm not leaving," she said again.

"Mason isn't lying, Bailey," the other detective reiterated. "What you're doing is extremely dangerous." He paused, but she simply nodded. She'd been hearing about the danger from the moment she first met O'Neill two nights ago, and wondered if she'd ever become immune to it. Somehow, she didn't think so.

Blake opened a small box and produced a thin credit card–shaped object with two copper wires attached to the ends. "You'll be wired for sound and location," he said, handing it to her. "We'll be close by in a surveillance van. Two, maybe more, other undercover officers will be nearby on the street. We're going to take every precaution to protect you, but as my partner has so eloquently pointed out, there are risks, and things can go wrong. If Shore asks you to leave with him, we'll be right behind you."

She examined the wire. It was hard plastic, a little deeper than flesh tone in color. "Won't Shore have me searched and find this?"

"There's every possibility he'll search you," Blake said with a nod, "but his chances of discovering the wire are highly doubtful."

"I don't understand."

Blake took the wire from her. "You wear this in your bra, under your breast. Unless he strips you down, the chances of it being discovered are minimal."

All she could think about was *who* was going to wire her. Memories of O'Neill's hands against her body swamped her. "Oh," she said for lack of a better response.

The object of her sensual thoughts dropped into the chair opposite her. Her gaze flew to his hands. Her body temperature rose a few degrees.

"You're not to leave with anyone except Shore," Blake said. "Provided you catch his attention, and we're sure you will, we expect him to send the Butcher to you first. You're to decline and ask to speak to Shore."

"The Butcher?" she asked, dragging her gaze away from O'Neill's large hands.

"Shore's number one henchman," O'Neill said. "He used to run drugs for Shore through the meat-packing plants in southeast Los Angeles, but he's been elevated to Shore's second in command. You'll know him the minute you see him. He's about two hundred and fifty pounds. Bald as a cue ball with a jagged scar over his left eye."

"How do you know this Butcher person will even let me near Shore?"

"He will," O'Neill said. There was a coldness in his voice that sent a shiver racing down her spine. "Trust me."

"How do you know?" she asked again, apprehension churning her stomach.

"She needs to know, Mason," Blake said. At O'Neill's nod, Blake continued. "Shore's been selling women, and not just by the hour. It's rumored the Butcher handpicks the girls for Shore."

"You mean like call girls?" She wasn't as naive as the two of them believed, although her knowledge was based on what she'd seen in movies through the years. And she was fairly certain the Hollywood version was light-years away from reality.

"No, Bailey," O'Neill said. "White slavery."

"Oh my God," she whispered. She stared at him, unable to believe what she was hearing. "But that's so…" The thought of buying and selling women was too appalling. "Are you sure?"

"No," Blake said. "And that's what we need you to confirm."

The import of what they were telling her hit home. "My God. Leslie." Fear snaked up her spine and settled coldly around her heart. The thought of her sister involved with Devlin Shore was frightening in and of itself, but nothing compared to the stark fear of what her sister must be experiencing.

She stood, needing to move, to do something. Unable to sit still, she paced the dining area. If only she'd sent for Leslie when she'd first called. If only she'd taken a leave of absence and returned to Whitewater when Leslie asked her, begged her, to return home. Leslie was in danger, and if they didn't hurry, she might never see her sister again.

She paced to the window and stopped. Heat rose in waves over the smog-filled city in the distance. Leslie was out there, somewhere, frightened and alone. They had to succeed. There was no other acceptable resolution.

She turned to face them. O'Neill looked grim. Blake's eyes held compassion. She didn't deserve his compassion. Leslie was in danger because of her.

"We've heard rumors on the streets that he finds the girls here, then sells them to buyers overseas. But we haven't got anything solid," Blake explained. "If we can get you on the inside, you might be able to find something, anything, that will give us the evidence we need to bring Shore down."

She wrapped her arms around her middle in an attempt to hold the fear inside. "I thought I was just going in to find my sister. And now you're telling me she could've already been sold to...to a..." She shook her head and looked away. "I just can't believe what I'm hearing."

"Believe it, Bailey," O'Neill's voice held none of the empathy of his partner's. "Ready to change your mind and let us do our job?"

Bailey looked at O'Neill, knowing she couldn't give him the answer he wanted. She had to do whatever necessary to find Leslie, no matter the cost. "I'm going to find my sister." She returned to the table and sat. "When are we going out?" she asked Blake.

"Tomorrow night."

Her eyes widened. "So soon?"

"We don't have much time. We don't know where Shore is holding the girls he sells." Blake reached across the table and laid his hand over hers. "We need that location, Bailey."

She pulled in a deep breath, summoning the tenacity that had brought her this far. O'Neill was right. What she was doing was dangerous. But she'd been prepared to go it alone. At least now she had the Los Angeles Police Department behind her.

"I'll do it," she said pulling her hand from Blake's. "I'll find out the location *and* my sister, if it's the last thing I ever do."

O'Neill leaned back in his chair and crossed his arms over his chest. He stared at her, the intensity in his eyes making her wary.

"Let's hope it's not," he said, the coldness in his voice matching the chill that had settled around her heart.

AFTER RECEIVING Bailey's promise not to reveal her whereabouts or any part of their plan to apprehend Shore and secure her sister's safety, Mason patched a call through the department so Bailey could telephone home. He didn't seriously believe her mother's phone would be bugged by Shore, but there was no excuse for sloppiness at this stage of the game.

Only they weren't playing a game. They were preparing to infiltrate the lair of one mean and ruthless S.O.B. who placed no value on human life.

Mason strode back into the dining area as Blake was clearing the table. His frustration level hadn't ebbed. He had a bad feeling, a deep-in-his-gut kind of twisting that warned him something was going to go drastically wrong. They needed more time to prepare Bailey. Two days was hardly enough for her to learn how to defend herself, and how to wear a wire without revealing it. But they didn't have much time. Tomorrow night they'd hit the streets, and they had to be ready. *She* had to be ready.

Hell, he'd had years of experience and had lived through the danger firsthand too many times to count. His stint as a Navy SEAL had taught him about danger and control. When he'd first joined the police force, he'd seen two of his fellow officers die in a shoot-out with a couple of punks who'd robbed a downtown bank. Emotion had been equally responsible for their deaths, since the younger officer's pregnant wife had been an employee at the bank targeted for robbery. He'd learned then that emotion was just as deadly as the perps they faced every day on the streets. He knew to expect that any scenario could blow up in their faces, but he had the experience and strong survival instinct required to keep him alive. Bailey was a civilian. An accountant. She'd lived her life in small-town America. Apparently the biggest risk she'd ever taken had been moving away from home, and that was hardly the kind of life experience that bred strong survival instincts.

As much as he'd argued with her and attempted to bully her into leaving, he realized if he wanted to bring Shore down, she was really the best chance they had right now. They had no hard evidence, only gut instinct. She'd been right. Shore had eluded them for far too long. He thought himself above the law, and eventually he'd make a mistake and they'd nail him. But how many more people had to die before that happened? While Mason hated the idea of her anywhere near Devlin Shore and his cronies, he told himself it was only because he feared if her true identity was discovered, it could mean the end of her life. There was every possibility that history might repeat itself, but was he really willing to let her go when they were so close?

He didn't like the answer.

"You planning to fit her with the wire tonight?" Blake asked, tucking the surveillance tool into the protective box.

He nodded, then took the box from Blake and laid it on the counter. "Tonight, before we go back into the gym." Earlier, he'd nearly lost the tight rein he kept on his control. This time he planned to keep his hands off her.

Blake straightened and shoved his hands into the pockets of his trousers. "Mason, you need to lighten up on her."

Mason scowled at his partner. "Someone has to make sure she's ready. She refuses to see the danger."

Blake sighed and shook his head. "You're wrong. She can see the danger, but her devotion to her sister is driving her. Take it easy on her, buddy."

"Take it easy on her?" Mason snapped. "That's rich coming from you, Hammond. You were there.

You saw what Shore did to the last civilian we used to draw him out in the open. Or did you listen to the department shrink when he told you to 'move on'?"

"Bailey isn't Ashley Adams," Blake said, ignoring Mason's biting sarcasm. "She's here willingly. She wants to do this, and she'll be prepared. She'll follow our instructions."

"You don't know that," Mason argued. "You don't know how she's going to react once this gets rolling. She has to be ready."

"Look, I know it was tough on you. I know you pushed for Ashley to help you and Jim Evers set up Shore, but things go wrong."

"Exactly why Bailey needs to be prepared for anything."

"You can't keep blaming yourself, Mason. You've got to let it go."

Mason seethed at Blake's Psych 101 mentality. Let it go? He'd tried. Lord knew he'd been trying for nearly three years, but he still woke up in the middle of the night with his body bathed in sweat.

"Losing a partner is always rough," Blake said, "and you and Jim Evers went back a long way. But you've got this single-minded drive to bring Shore down and make him pay for Jim and Ashley. It's going to get you killed, Mason. What kind of help will you be to Bailey then?"

Mason planted his hands on his hips and glared at Blake. Was his partner actually implying he'd lost his focus? "Shore's a cop killer. Doesn't that mean anything to you?" It sure as hell meant everything to Mason.

A hardness rarely seen entered his partner's

eyes. "Yeah, it does," Blake said slowly, choosing his words carefully. "But you're obsessed. And that's more dangerous than what we're asking Bailey to do."

Mason looked at Blake in disbelief. Obsessed? Hardly. More like determined to see the cop killer behind bars.

"Look," Blake said, "Bailey's going through her own personal hell right now. A blind man could see the guilt she's feeling. You want to keep her alive? Then take it easy on her. You keep driving her this way and you're going to be sorry."

"Emotions have no place in a situation like this," Mason retorted.

Blake rocked back on his heels and continued to stare at Mason. "Then what's your excuse?" he asked sarcastically.

Mason crossed his arms over his chest. "What are you getting at, Hammond? You saying that I'm losing my edge?"

"No," Blake answered. "But...there's something going on between you and Bailey. You get involved with her, it could get you both killed."

"There's nothing going on."

Blake straightened the reports he'd left on the table and set them inside the manila file folder he'd brought with him. The file labeled Shore.

"Sure, partner," he said, tossing the file on the counter beside the box holding the wire. "Whatever you say. Just remember what you said—emotions have no place in a situation like this. And if you're falling for Bailey Grayson, then you'd be wise to let someone else supervise this operation."

"Like hell. Shore is mine," he said coldly. The

bastard *was* his. There was a score to settle. And he wouldn't rest until he had the scum behind bars where he belonged.

"And Bailey?"

"Don't worry about Bailey."

"Someone has to," Blake said. "Because you're getting involved."

Mason said nothing as Blake strode past him and headed toward the door. He wasn't "getting involved" with Bailey. There was a serious case of lust happening, but nothing more. She was a decent person with a deep sense of loyalty to those she loved. And he was going to do his best to ensure she lived to see those loved ones again.

He shoved a hand through his hair in frustration. He was *not* falling for Bailey. His partner was seeing things that weren't there. And his "obsession" as Blake called it, would not get him, or Bailey, killed.

Not on his watch.

"And Bailey?"

7

MASON SPREAD more of the marinade Bailey had
made over the chicken breasts before snapping the
grill lid closed. His mood hadn't improved, and
when Bailey first suggested they use the outdoor
grill and enjoy what they could of the evening, he'd
scoffed. They weren't playing house. But he'd re-
lented, and still hadn't come up with a plausible
explanation as to why he'd agreed, other than he
was tired of microwave or fast-food meals. It had
been a long time since he'd had a home-cooked
meal. Two years in fact.

He dropped into a lounge chair on the patio and
crossed his feet at the ankles. Bracing his elbows on
the chair, he laid his hands over his stomach and
watched Bailey through the wide kitchen window,
her head bent over some task. He wanted to blame
her for his foul mood, and although he did hold her
responsible in some small degree, he was beginning to think it had little to do with her idiotic determination to put her life in danger, and more
with the truth Blake had shoved down his throat.

A truth that indeed something was going on between him and Bailey.

What he was feeling didn't have so much to do
with her status as a plant, but as a woman. A
woman who made him wonder what the future

held, and think about his past. A past darkened by a marriage riddled with failures. His failures.

Mason stood and opened the lid on the grill to turn the chicken, then brushed more marinade over the browning meat. He decided he didn't want to think about the past, or his failed marriage to Karen, but he couldn't stop the thoughts from running through his mind. Two years ago when she'd first left him and taken their son, Cody, back to Chicago, he'd been angry. So angry that he'd called her selfish. He'd moved away from his family, left the Chicago Police Department where three generations of O'Neill men had served, to follow her to Los Angeles. During their argument the night she left him, she told him that she'd requested the transfer to California hoping that by doing so, they could save a marriage that had already been in trouble. He'd never realized that anything was wrong until it was too late.

He recalled too many missed meals, neatly covered with plastic wrap waiting for him in the refrigerator. At first there'd been little notes attached. They'd started out flirtatious, then more to the point, indicating simply that she'd missed him. Before long, the notes had disappeared altogether.

He thought about the early mornings he'd crept into a quiet house after sitting on a stakeout all night, and how he'd been too beat to notice her tight-lipped silence because he'd missed Cody's parent-teacher conference, Little League game or science fair. He remembered too many late nights and many more angry silences because he'd forgotten about a gathering with friends or an evening of dinner and drinks with a client she'd been attempting to woo to the advertising firm where she worked as an account manager.

Rather than looking at his own failings, he'd mistakenly thought Karen demanding, but with the clarity of hindsight, he realized all she had wanted was a husband. One who put his family first, and the job second.

The year following the deaths of his partner and the civilian remained a blur. He'd become driven then, so single-minded in bringing Shore to justice that everything else had taken a back seat. He'd continuously forsaken the two most important people in his life: Karen and Cody. He'd sacrificed his family. And for what?

Alone, in the dark hours of the night when sleep eluded him, the answer was clear, and difficult to face. His hunger for vengeance was all-consuming. During the light of day, it was easier to hide from the truth behind his badge.

The sliding glass door opened and Bailey stepped out into the evening sunshine with Jo running alongside her. The light breeze rustling the leaves on the trees stirred her rich blond hair, but did little to cool the temperature that had risen past the century mark long ago. She wore a cropped blue T-shirt that brushed the waistband of her white shorts. She looked young and untouched by life's cruelty. A stern reminder she'd never be equipped to hold her own against someone like Devlin Shore.

Since she'd agreed to act as a plant, he'd bullied her, argued with her and bluntly told her exactly what Shore was capable of doing. None of that mattered to her. She was as single-minded as he was, and twice as stubborn.

She came up beside him, a glass of lemonade in her hands. She smelled of sunshine and flowers and woman. "I thought you might want something to drink. It isn't fresh-squeezed, but not half-bad."

"Thanks," he said, taking the glass. She wiped the condensation from her hands by sliding them along her hips. He followed the movement with his eyes, quickly imagining his own hands gliding over her hips, and lower. "The chicken's almost ready."

"Great. I'm starved." She turned one of the lawn chairs away from the harsh glare of the evening sun and sat. "I made some potatoes and a salad."

He returned to the chair he'd been sitting in earlier and motioned for Jo to join him. The large dog groaned and laid on the concrete by Bailey's feet, instead. "Whatever," he said, giving the dog a skeptical glance. "I'm easy."

Bailey's eyes filled with humor. "Sure you are, O'Neill. And Attila the Hun was just a misunderstood tyrant."

He leaned forward and looked at her, bracing his elbows on his knees. "Look, I know you think I'm a jerk, but I don't like using civilians."

She shrugged, a simple movement that inched up her top, giving him a peak at her lightly tanned skin. "I'm trying not to take it personally."

The humor he'd detected earlier extinguished, unmasking the resoluteness he was becoming accustomed to in her eyes. "You should," he told her harshly. "It's not only your life that's going to be on the line, but several officers', as well as your sister's. You need to take it *very* personally."

She pulled her legs up and wrapped her slender arms around them, hugging them close to her chest. "O'Neill, I know the dangers. You're not going to change my mind."

"I don't think you realize exactly how dangerous—"

"I know enough. Just drop it. Please. I don't want to argue anymore."

He stood and opened the lid on the grill. He, too, was tired of arguing. Nothing he'd tried had changed her mind, and she'd stubbornly held her ground. Blake had told him to lighten up on her. That he couldn't do. If she was determined to continue, then he had no choice but to make damn sure she was capable of handling herself.

He transferred the chicken from the grill to the serving platter she'd brought out earlier. "Let's eat," he said, shutting down the barbecue.

She rose and followed him into the house, holding the door open for Jo. While Bailey delivered twice-baked potatoes and salad to the table, the dog located a strategic position between them, clearly hoping for an opportunity of table scraps.

They ate in silence, each concentrating on the meal. "This is good," he finally said, adding another ladle of dressing to his salad.

Bailey sliced a tomato wedge in half and stabbed it with her fork. "My mom liked to cook. I paid attention."

"What was it like?" he asked, not because he was interested, he told himself, but anything was better than the heavy silence surrounding them. "Living on a farm, I mean."

She reached across the table for the pepper. "We had a dairy farm," she said, sprinkling her food liberally. "It's a little different than other kinds of farms."

"Meaning?" he asked between bites of the most heavenly chicken he'd tasted in years. Bailey was some cook, he thought, and couldn't help wondering about her other hidden talents.

She carefully cut the grilled chicken breast into bite-size cubes. "Produce farmers work year-round, but their busiest times are the planting and harvesting seasons. You're pretty much married to dairy farming. The cows have to be tended to constantly. There aren't any vacations, or days off."

"Is that why you left? Because you wanted vacations and days off?" He could understand, considering his own dedication to the job. Perps didn't take vacations or days off, either. Crime happened twenty-four hours a day, seven days a week.

She shrugged a slim shoulder. "Partly," she said, then turned her attention back to the food on her plate. "So why'd you become a cop?"

"Family tradition," he said without hesitation, helping himself to another chicken breast. There'd never been another choice for him. He'd grown up knowing he was going to become a peace officer, just like his father and his father's father. By the time Mason had graduated from high school, his oldest brother, Tony, had already joined the force. And Mike, two years older than Mason, was preparing to enter the academy just having graduated from a two-year college in South Bend. Even his youngest brother, Tim, had joined the force three years ago. Two months before Mason graduated from high school, he'd already enlisted in the navy, with plans to join the SEALs, sure in the knowledge that once his stint in the service ended, he'd attend the academy and earn his shield. But Karen had told him she was pregnant the week before he was scheduled to leave for San Diego. Never one to shirk his responsibilities, he'd married her, but left her behind with her family and marched off to boot camp.

Bailey sipped her lemonade. She knew about family traditions and expectations. She'd broken the mold herself, first by going to college when she'd been expected to stay in Whitewater, find a nice marriageable boy and raise a few children along with a few cows. Instead, she'd moved away and hadn't looked back. "How long have you been with the L.A.P.D.?"

"Five years," he said. "I started out in Chicago with my old man and brothers. An O'Neill has been in the Chicago P.D. for three generations. I broke rank when my ex-wife received a transfer to L.A. I wrangled a lateral move and have been here ever since."

He held out a piece of chicken to Jo, who gently took it from his hand. "My ex moved back to Chicago three years ago with our son. He's almost thirteen," he said, patting the dog's head.

"Do you have a picture of him?"

Mason grinned and shifted in his seat, retrieving his wallet. He flipped it open and handed it to her. She smiled at the dark-haired boy who instantly reminded her of Mason, primarily due to the stubborn glint in the boy's dark blue eyes.

"He's cute," she said, handing him back the wallet. "I bet he misses you."

He dropped the wallet on the table. "I miss Cody, too. Pictures and phone calls are a poor substitute for spending time with my son."

"You don't see him often?"

"Not as much as I'd like. I make sure I call him at least once a week, and Karen sends him out for a month every summer, but it's tough to maintain a solid relationship."

Her heart went out to Mason. As much as she complained about living in a small town where everyone knew everyone else's business, at least she'd been fortunate and had both of her parents.

They finished their meal by exchanging stories of their childhoods. She was struck by the differences, yet there were similarities, as well. She might have been raised in a place where doors remained unlocked, while O'Neill had spent his childhood on the mean streets of Chicago, but it was obvious he felt a strong sense of community toward his neighborhood back in Chicago. She couldn't wait to escape rural America and the people she'd known all her life, who knew everything about her and she them. At times she missed that security, but for the most part, she appreciated her independence. Although he didn't say so, she could tell by the tone of his voice and the way his honey gold eyes filled with longing that he often thought of the family he'd left behind. The difference was, she'd be returning to Whitewater not because she wanted to, but because of duty to her family.

She gathered their plates and carried them to the sink. "Why are you still in L.A.? I mean, it sounds like you really miss Illinois."

She turned around in time to see his gaze harden. "Once I bring down Shore and he's behind bars, then I'll think about transferring back to Chicago."

She understood his determination, and sensed something else that he wasn't telling her. There was more to this thing with Devlin Shore, she was sure of it.

He carried the few remaining dishes into the kitchen and set them on the counter. The hardness disappeared from his eyes and he looked at her speculatively. "You know, you don't strike me as the stuffy accountant type."

She began rinsing the dishes and started handing them to O'Neill to place inside the dishwasher. "Thanks. I'll take that as a compliment, I think," she said with a smile, holding out another plate. "My dad taught me how to do the books one summer, and I just took to it. After that, accounting seemed like a logical career choice."

He set the plate in the dishwasher and waited for another. "No man in your life?"

Did she really detect a brusqueness in his voice, or was she imagining things? Imagining things, she decided. "Not really. I work and go home to my apartment. I have a few friends in the city, but I'm pretty much a hermit. It's the long hours."

"I know about long hours," he said, arranging the silverware in the holder.

She rinsed out the dishrag and started wiping down the tiled countertop. "I'm not really attracted to those 'stuffy accountant types.'"

"What kind are you attracted to?" he asked, closing the door to the dishwasher. He propped his hip against the counter and looked at her, causing her insides to flutter again.

Grumpy detectives, she thought, but kept that revelation to herself. She didn't think O'Neill would appreciate knowing she had the hots for him. Okay, so he probably knew based on her earlier behavior, but that didn't mean she had to announce it, did she? Instead of answering him, she rinsed the rag, then folded it over the sink divider.

He moved away, thankfully not pushing the issue. Not that she'd admit anything to him. They were in an intense situation and emotions were bound to run high. Her judgment was skewed because of the danger they were facing, nothing more.

Oh, sure, she was attracted to O'Neill. Who wouldn't be attracted to him? The man represented power and strength, not to mention that he was more good-looking than any man she'd ever known. But she realized that the intensity of emotion she felt toward O'Neill was created by the threat of danger. Once the danger ended, so would any relationship they might test during their time together. She might be innocent when it came to affairs with the opposite sex, but she wasn't foolish enough to believe she and O'Neill would even see each other again once their objectives were met: Shore behind bars, Leslie tucked safely in Whitewater. It would be mission accomplished, *hasta la bye-bye, baby*.

She could learn something from O'Neill other than basic self-defense techniques. She could learn from that iron will he tried so hard to maintain. She could learn not to be affected when he touched her, and how to shut off her emotions as effectively as he did. Otherwise, how could he have held her the way he had in the gym, kissed her as if she was the only woman in the world who meant anything to him and then act as if nothing had happened?

If he could do it, so could she.

Jo trotted over to the sliding door and sat quietly, looking over her shoulder at them. After a moment, she whined and thumped her tail on the terra-cotta tiles. O'Neill snagged a box from the counter, then opened the door for Jo.

Convincing herself she could, and would, remain unaffected from this moment forward, Bailey strolled into the spacious living room. The sun still rode low on the horizon, and she was far from tired. Rather than disappear to the safety of her bedroom, where she suspected she'd simply toss and turn for hours without falling asleep, she dropped onto the sofa and picked up the remote for the wide-screen television. Maybe she could find a movie to pass a few hours' time.

O'Neill sauntered into the room, the small cardboard box in his hand. "Take off your shirt," he said.

"Excuse me?" she squeaked. A dozen images filtered through her mind, and not a single one had anything to do with remaining unaffected by O'Neill. So much for her resolution of iron will.

"The wire," he said, sitting on the square coffee table in front of her. "You need to get used to wearing it so you're not moving around it."

"Moving around it?" *Take off your shirt*. Her stomach clenched.

"Ever notice how some street cops hold their arms away from their body?" he asked.

She nodded in response to his question, because she couldn't have found her voice with a road map and two hands.

Take off your shirt.

Oh, dear Lord, this iron-will thing was harder than she'd imagined.

"They're moving 'around' their weapon," O'Neill explained, removing the electronic device from the box. "The weapon isn't a part of them, so it's obvious they're carrying, even when the weapon isn't in plain sight. Same is true with wires. You get used to wearing it, you forget it's there. You move around it and someone with experience will know you're wired."

"Like Shore or his Butcher friend."

"Exactly. Now take off your shirt."

She searched his eyes and saw nothing out of the ordinary, nothing that said he was affected by his dispassionate request. The same wasn't true for her. Far from it, if she used her resulting tummy flutters as a barometer.

There is nothing sexual about this, she told herself. *O'Neill is simply doing his best to prepare me for tomorrow night*. She sucked in a deep breath, then reached for the hem of her cropped T-shirt. Slowly, she lifted the ends and slipped the shirt over her head. Her hands automatically moved to cover her breasts even though she was wearing a bra, but he reached out and stopped her, holding her hands in her lap.

She looked up at O'Neill. His eyes had darkened, and a muscle ticked in his jaw. Maybe he wasn't as unaffected as she wanted to think.

Never taking her eyes from his, she slowly pulled her hands from his grasp and reached for the front hook on her bra. She undid the clasp and took a deep breath, but the effort did nothing to stop the thundering of her heart. With aching slowness, she peeled the lace from her skin.

O'Neill ran his palms over his thighs and stifled a groan. With the wire in his shaking hand, he moved closer. Her tummy started to flutter again, and her nipples beaded. Her breasts felt achy and heavy, and supersensitive. Sweet heaven, she longed for his hands to caress her.

Her breathing deepened, and she felt as if she was locked in a trance. A trance created by the intensity of heat blazing in his eyes.

"Mason?" she questioned, not sure what was happening between them, but certain that he was going to kiss her again. He moved closer, slowly, his hand sliding over her rib cage to her back. He joined her on the sofa, then pressed her down, surrounding her with his body. The rough fabric of the sofa brushed against her back, a contrast to the smooth hardness of O'Neill pressed against her. She reveled in the scents, the textures, the feel of his hands on her bare skin, of his body moving seductively against her as he settled them into a more comfortable position. A shiver passed through her, but not from cold. Hardly from cold, she thought, because her body suddenly felt on fire.

His hand slipped between them to caress her breast. She sucked in a breath when his thumb brushed her distended nipple. His touch rasped against her sensitized skin and she arched toward his hand as another spiral of heat flared through her.

His mouth captured hers in one of those bone-melting kisses that set her soul on fire. A momentary thought of maintaining control filtered through her mind, but she quickly locked the door that led to common sense, too enraptured by the wild sensations coursing through her. She was playing with fire, but the fire was so much more pleasurable than she'd ever dreamed possible. It teased her, lured her, made her want things she didn't entirely understand. But she knew that wasn't completely true, it wasn't the fire licking through her—it was O'Neill.

When he shifted them again, he settled his body between her thighs. A bolt of electricity whipped through her like a live wire blown loose in a storm. She arched against him once more, her body seeking his instinctively. He groaned into her mouth, and she thought she'd never heard a more heavenly sound.

His mouth left hers, and she protested, despite the delicious wickedness his tongue created blazing a path along her jaw and down her throat to her breast. She moaned when he pulled a beaded nipple into his hot, wet mouth, then she brazenly slipped her hands through his hair to hold him in place. She never wanted him to stop his erotic exploration. Heat was curling throughout her body, racing through her veins at lightning speed. Never had she known such pleasure, but she welcomed the unknown. She was awestruck and swept away with sensation. All that mattered was O'Neill and the delicious way he made her feel.

He lifted his head and looked at her. His eyes were dark, the honey gold turning to a deep bronze. She recognized the desire flaring in his gaze now, and her breath caught.

"I want you, Bailey," he said. "God help me, I shouldn't, but I do."

Before she could respond, he settled his mouth over hers again, this time more insistent and demanding. She moaned in response as his tongue swept inside her mouth, tasting, laving, retreating then entering again to taste more deeply than before. She imagined him doing the same with their bodies, of him filling her, retreating, then filling her again as they made love. She'd never known a kiss could be so erotic, or that kissing could imitate the natural completion of their bodies. And God help *her*, she wanted O'Neill just as fiercely.

His hand left her breast and swept over her tummy to the waistband of her shorts. He undid the top snap, then snaked the zipper down. She had a brief thought of stopping him, but lifted her bottom instead so he could push the shorts from her hips. She wanted him, but failed to find an explanation any more than she could explain the theory of relativity. All she knew was that she was naked beneath him, only his clothes and her whisper-thin lace panties separated them. She wanted him in the most intimate way possible.

Analytical thought flew from her mind when his hand slipped beneath the lace edge of her panties to cup her intimately in his palm. She tensed slightly when he opened her and slipped his finger inside, but he deepened the kiss, forcing cognitive thought aside, allowing room for only pure feeling and sensation. The movement of his mouth matched that of his hand. The intensity built, making her feel tighter and tighter, until she was certain she would snap in two.

She needed, but had no clue what she needed, only that the pleasure he created with his hand and mouth, the building of something just out of her reach was making her mindless. He took her further, building her need, edging her closer to what, she didn't know, but she reached for it anyway, giving him her faith to keep her safe.

And then she fell over the edge, or rose toward the heavens, she couldn't be sure, but for the first time in her life, she tasted pure rapture. There weren't any fireworks, no bursting lights or crashing of waves. Yet the rush of pleasure was so intense she never felt more complete, or alive.

His mouth left hers and he rained kisses on her temple, her eyes and her lips, holding her close while she fell apart in his arms. She clung to him, trusting him to guide her gently back to earth.

As she waited for her breathing pattern to return to normal, she looked at O'Neill, the gentleness she'd always detected in him evident in his eyes and his touch. He cradled her against his chest and she pulled in a deep breath, reveling in his scent.

"I never knew it could be like this," she whispered. She'd never dreamed such wicked pleasure could be derived simply from a man's touch.

He chuckled, smoothing her hair away from her face. He kissed her again, long and slow, lingering and deep.

Abruptly, he ended the kiss and pulled back. "What do you mean?" he asked, eyeing her with caution.

Suddenly shy, she felt heat creep into her cheeks. "That making love could be so beautiful."

She knew the instant he realized the truth because he practically recoiled from her. He pushed off her and sat, staring at her. The gentleness had disappeared, replaced by the hard-edged O'Neill, confusing her. How could he love her so tenderly, bring her to such pleasure, then act as if she was a pariah?

She reached for her bra and T-shirt, fighting to hold on to what dignity she had left. She would *not* cry in front of him.

"What are you saying, Bailey?" he asked, his voice as hard as his stare was cold.

She slipped her shirt over her head, then searched the cushions for her shorts. Tears blurred her vision, but she managed to locate her shorts and slip them on before facing him. Clothed, she didn't feel so exposed, but she knew that was a lie. She'd never felt more exposed or raw than she did at this very moment.

She lifted her chin and straightened her shoulders. Giving him a level stare, she answered him as calmly as she could manage, given the circumstances and her complete and total humiliation.

"I've never made love to a man," she said.

When he said nothing, she spun on her heel and exited the room through the sliding glass door. She closed the door behind her, but not before she heard Mason's ripe and very succinct curse.

8

MASON SUCKED in deep breaths, waiting for his heart rate to resume a normal pace. Not many things shocked or surprised him, but Bailey had thrown him a curveball he hadn't seen coming. And it had landed with perfect precision right in his lap.

I've never made love to a man.

He blew out a stream of breath filled with frustration. How was it possible she'd remained untouched all these years? Ten minutes ago he'd wanted nothing more than to make her his, to imprint himself on her soul. Surely he wasn't the only man who'd ever felt that way about her. How had she remained a…a… Damn, he couldn't even bring himself to think the word.

He left the sofa and strode to the sliding glass door. She stood on the edge of the patio with her back to the house, giving him the opportunity to view her unobserved. Impossible, he thought. She was sexier than any number of women he knew. Hell, in this day and age, anyone over the age of eighteen had usually made love at least once, and more often than not, they'd done it for the first time in the back seat of a Chevy. How was it that such a beautiful, sexy young woman had escaped that natural progression? Surely some guy would have tasted her special, erotic brand of passion by now.

Obviously not.

He didn't believe her "status" had anything to do with unresponsiveness or disinterest in sex. She'd been totally responsive in *his* arms, and not the least bit virginal. She hadn't shied away from the things they'd done. Instead, she'd fallen apart in his arms, hiking his male pride more than a few notches that she'd done so with only his touch.

"A virgin," he muttered under his breath. Maybe that explained the sweetness about her that drew him. Maybe that explained his wanting to protect her and keep her safe. Or maybe he wanted her, knowing on some unconscious level that he'd be her first and someone she'd never forget.

God, and he'd acted like a total jerk. But he'd been so shocked—especially when his only thought had been to make love to her.

He shoved his hand through his hair, then braced his arm on the wall above his head. Her shoulders heaved, as if she'd just been crying. She kept her arms wrapped around her middle as she gazed at the city below and the lights twinkling in the dusk-covered distance. Her face was obscured by the twilight, but he sincerely hoped her tears had abated. He didn't need the moist reminder that he'd behaved like a first-class jerk.

He needed to talk to her. To reassure her that his reaction had nothing to do with her, but with the shock she'd given him. He only hoped he could make her understand, because the last thing he wanted to do was hurt her further.

Quietly, he slid open the door and stepped out

into the balmy night. Twilight brought a light breeze inland from the ocean, cooling the California night. He moved behind her, gently laying his hands over her shoulders. She stiffened, but didn't move away. He took that as a positive sign.

"I'm sorry," he said quietly.

She nodded, and he wondered if she was still crying or simply refused to speak to him. He wouldn't blame her if she never spoke to him again...except the purpose of their association forbade silence. Communication was important. Their lives depended on it.

Gently, he massaged her shoulders, his fingers brushing the exposed skin at the nape of her neck. Skin that still felt like silk beneath his hands. "You, uh...took me by surprise."

She sniffled and swiped the moisture from her eyes with the back of her hand. "You must think I'm a freak," she said, her voice a choked whisper that chipped at his heart.

"No. I don't," he answered with sincerity. Sure, she'd given him one hell of a shock, but a freak? Never. She was intelligent, beautiful, sexy, and despite her surprising revelation, he still wanted her. He wanted her with a ferocity that unnerved him. But she was off-limits. She was a means to an end, nothing more.

He didn't believe that any more than he believed in Santa Claus, the Easter Bunny or the Tooth Fairy.

"How many twenty-four-year-old virgins do you know? We aren't exactly the norm," she quipped.

"In my line of work, not too many."

She made a sound that bordered on a caustic little laugh or one of self-disgust. He opted for caustic.

"Okay, none," he said, a grin curving his lips.

She sighed and moved away from him. Stepping up to the wrought-iron railing, she wrapped her hands around the edge and leaned forward. He had a perfect view of her curvy behind and lithe, tanned legs. His imagination jumped into high gear as he thought of those legs wrapped around his waist. Good God, he wanted her. He wanted her bad.

She looked over her shoulder at him, and he dragged his gaze from her derriere to her face. A light frown marred her forehead, and her eyes glistened with moisture. "I should have said something sooner. I'm sorry."

He approached her, turned and propped his backside against the railing before crossing his feet at the ankles. Using his hands to support himself, he leaned back to get a good look at her face. Her eyes were red-rimmed from crying. Dammit, he'd done that to her, and he hated himself for it.

"Yeah, you should have," he said. "I never would have let things go so far if I'd known."

She frowned. "Not into deflowering virgins, eh? You like your women with a little more experience, is that it?"

He scowled at her sarcasm. "That's not what I meant."

She pushed off the railing and leveled her gaze on him. "Then what did you mean, O'Neill? You know, you *were* a willing participant back in that living room. You had no problem..." she stalled, a becoming blush staining her cheeks. She cleared her throat. "You had no problem... It didn't bother you until you found out it was my first time. Why is it such a big deal now?"

He suspected the dent in her feminine pride caused by his putting an abrupt halt to their love-making stung more than any possible embarrassment over his discovering she was untouched. Reaching for her, he pulled her close, settling her between his legs. Using his finger, he lifted her chin until she looked at him. "Your first time should be special," he said gently. "Not a groping session on a sofa in a safe house with a virtual stranger."

She crossed her arms over her chest, the frown returning. "What makes you think it wouldn't be special? Oh, wait, I get it. Forgive me for being so naive. You know us virgins, we don't get around much. I'd just be one more in an obviously long line of participants in the mattress Olympics."

He dropped his hand from her chin and matched her frown with one of his own. "Dammit, Bailey, that's not what I'm talking about and you know it."

"What I know is that I wanted to make love to you, O'Neill, and the minute you found out that I'd never been with a man before, you...you..." Tears filled her eyes again.

"Rejected you?" he finished for her when she stepped away.

He hadn't wanted to hurt her, but he had, and he'd apologized for that. But he was not sorry he hadn't followed the natural progression of their lovemaking and completed what they'd started. Oh, he wanted to make love to her, he wanted nothing more than to carry her off to bed and make love to her all night long, exhausting them both. So much so that he was still aching with need and desire.

At her nod, he said, "I don't want the responsibility. Don't you think the first man you make love to should be someone special?"

She looked at him, tears brimming in her eyes. "Yes, I do," she said quietly.

Her words hit him like a wet lash to bare skin, searing his soul, and his mind. Something tugged at him, deep inside, but he fought against it. "I'm no one special, Bailey. I'm just the guy who's helping you find your sister. That's all. Don't confuse gratitude with something that doesn't exist between us."

She pulled in a shaky breath and returned to the railing. Leaning forward, she lifted her face to the night sky. The cricket serenade and the soft rustle of leaves in the trees disturbed the heavy silence between them.

"You want me to believe I'm just an available body and you're ready, willing and able to do the job," she said quietly, her attention still on the stars. She turned and shot him a knowing look. "I can't buy that, O'Neill. You wanted me."

"There's a difference between wanting someone and loving them," he said. He couldn't deny her claim. He had wanted her. He still did, and that annoyed him. He knew her type. She wanted a knight in shining armor. He might have some armor stashed somewhere in his checkered past, but it was too tarnished to be of any use now.

Impatience crossed her face. "Who said anything about love? I'm talking *need*, O'Neill. *Desire*," she admitted, her voice laced with frustration.

"You don't even know me," he argued.

She released an exaggerated huff. "I know enough. I know you're not the tough guy you want everyone to believe. You're a very caring man."

He crossed his arms over his chest and glared at her. She didn't know anything about him. If she suspected the truth, they certainly wouldn't be having this conversation, because she'd want nothing to do with him, and she certainly wouldn't be depending on him to save her sister from Devlin Shore's clutches. "You don't know what you're talking about."

A wry grin flirted around the corners of her mouth. "Oh, Mason," she said, shaking her head. "You're not so tough. I admit it, I was confused at first. I thought, 'What's a tough guy like you doing with such a sweet dog, and one who's obviously way past her prime?' So I asked your partner, and you know what he told me?"

"Don't stop now," he said sarcastically.

"He told me she'd been badly wounded in the line of duty and the department was going to have her put down. He told me *you*, Mr. Tough Guy, intervened and saved her life. She's here with us now because you won't even put her in a kennel."

His gaze sought out the dog in question. Jo lay sprawled near the barbecue, snoring softly. "So I like animals," he said, turning his attention back to Bailey. She grinned. He deepened his frown in response. "What's the big deal?"

She laughed, a light sound that teased his senses. "The big deal is you care. And you care about your family. I could see it in your eyes when you talked about them tonight at dinner. Face it, O'Neill. You're really a marshmallow inside."

"That's bull."

She shook her head in bemusement. "It's the truth. You're nowhere near the callous bastard you want me to believe you are."

"So I've got a soft spot for dogs and family," he said with a shrug. "That doesn't mean squat."

Locking her gaze with his, she stepped forward. Slowly, she reached up and smoothed her hand over his cheek. Her touch was light, gentle and made him wish things could be different between them.

"Yes, it does, O'Neill," she said, her voice as light and soft as her touch. "It means that all your bullying to get me to leave isn't all because you don't want to work with an amateur. You care. And that's enough for me."

He grasped her wrist to keep her from touching him. If she wasn't careful, he might just relent and take the precious gift she so willingly offered, regardless of the heartache he'd end up causing her.

"You're wrong," he said. "I *don't* want to work with an amateur. When all this comes down, and it will, it's going to get hot, and you're going to panic. It's nothing personal, but you're dangerous, to yourself, to the other officers you'll be working with and to your sister."

She shook her head. "You don't know that."

"Yes, I do," he said. He knew firsthand how one wrong move could lead them right into disaster. "I'm stuck with you. Whether I like it or not."

"I'll be ready."

He didn't doubt her resolve, or her sincerity. But it changed nothing.

"You'd better be," he said, releasing her hand. "Tomorrow night we hit the streets, and you'd better pray you *are* ready. Because there'll be no turning back once we start."

BAILEY PULLED her legs beneath her and cuddled with the Southwestern throw she'd brought with her from the bedroom. A pair of leather recliners faced a stone hearth, and she'd chosen the one closest to the window so she could look up at the stars. The fireplace was a much larger version of the one she'd had in her childhood home in Whitewater. She sat now, the room bathed in moonlight, the midnight sky forgotten as she stared into the cold hearth, remembering one particularly chilly autumn night when she'd been thirteen or fourteen. Her mother had insisted her father build a cozy fire, and together they'd all roasted marshmallows, while her mother had made them S'mores using cinnamon graham crackers and her special stash of white-chocolate bars.

Long after she and Leslie had gone to bed, Bailey had crept downstairs for a glass of milk. She could still remember the shock of discovering her parents lying before the fire, a blanket covering their bodies and their clothes thrown into a pile in the corner. She'd stood mesmerized as her parents clung to each other watching the fire, sharing tender kisses amid whispered words of love.

As she'd crept back to bed, careful not to disturb them, she realized that she'd never wanted to be like Lisa Scott or Patty Jackson, who went all the way with the boys at Whitewater High School. She didn't want people talking about her the way they talked about Lisa and Patty. Nor did she want to be known as one of "those" girls people snickered about or the old matrons in town glared at when they walked by. What she wanted was to be special, to one person, to one man, just as her mother was to her father.

She sighed. For so long she'd thought it had been her mother's constant lectures on how a lady behaves, or good girls don't let boys do this to them or that to them. But now, with the understanding that came with maturity, she realized what she'd wanted all along was to be special to that one certain man, the one with whom she'd spend the rest of her life.

She'd wanted love, not lust.

Until she'd met O'Neill.

What was it about him that had her giving serious consideration to tossing aside those lofty aspirations she'd developed at a young age, and had turned into her own moral code of honor? Why did it have to be him that her body craved? And how on earth could she have fallen for someone she hardly knew?

And there lay the crux of her dilemma. She'd always suspected that she'd know when the right man came along. She'd had dates, even a couple of serious boyfriends, but she'd never once experienced that wild beating of her heart, never felt fire race through her veins from a single touch, never felt her knees go weak from a simple glance. Never had she daydreamed about making love with any of them.

Only O'Neill.

Like a fool, she'd thrown herself at him. And stubborn cuss that he was, he'd rejected her. She knew he wanted her. Knew it deep in her heart and felt it in the marrow of her bones. He'd touched more than her skin, he'd touched her heart.

The wire still lay on the cocktail table where they'd left it hours before. She reached forward and plucked it off the table. After unfastening the buttons on her nightie, she made several attempts to adjust the wire as Detective Hammond had explained, but couldn't grasp where the two copper wires would lie.

She heard the creak of a door and straightened, pulling the blanket up to her chin. She sat quietly, watching the hallway, waiting for O'Neill to appear. He did, and she stifled a sharp gasp.

Moonlight from the open window illuminated his body. He looked raw, untamed, every inch of him male. Shirtless, she admired his broad, bare chest before allowing her gaze to drop to discover a pair of fleece shorts riding low on his hips. His stomach was lean and muscular, and she ached to trace the outline of his ribs beneath his solid flesh. She continued her admiring perusal down to his muscular thighs. A shiver of delight coursed through her as she remembered the feel of his thighs pressed intimately against hers.

Her gaze drifted leisurely back to his face in time to see him frown suddenly. He peered into the semidarkness, as if he sensed he was no longer alone.

"I'm over here," she said quietly.

"What are you doing up?" he asked, his frown deepening.

"I couldn't sleep."

He reached for the light switch, but she stopped him. "I prefer the darkness."

He shrugged, then moved to the other recliner. He sat on the edge and faced her. "You should be in bed. Tomorrow's going to be a tough day."

The only bed she wanted to be in right now was O'Neill's, but she didn't think he'd want to hear about that. "Did I wake you?"

"I couldn't sleep, either."

"Gee, O'Neill," she teased, hoping to lighten the mood. "People are going to think we have something in common if we're not careful."

He gave a soft chuckle that warmed her clear to her toes. When he smiled, when he let down the barriers even for a moment, she sometimes caught a glimpse of the man beneath the gruff exterior. That was the man she was falling for—the one who cared about those around him, the one who was dedicated to his job and believed in the motto "to protect and serve." That was the man who'd touched her deep inside and made her yearn for all the heart-stopping excitement of just being near him.

He frowned again, and looked at the cocktail table, then her. "Where's the wire?"

She blew out a stream of breath. "I was...uh... trying it on."

He nodded slowly, as if deciding whether or not he wanted to revisit the scenario that had led them to the most fulfilling and earth-shattering sexual experience of her life. Not that she'd mind a repeat performance, but based on his reaction, she'd have better luck selling ice cubes to the residents of the North Pole.

"I see," he said after a moment.

Silence settled around them once again, not an uncomfortable type of quiet where she searched frantically for something to say to fill the void. No, this was more companionable, cozy almost. Her imagination sparked. She envisioned them before a blazing hearth, a blanket covering their bodies as they clung to each other, both of them spent from lovemaking. Tender touches, and more tender words, followed by soul-reaching kisses.

She had to stop these foolish thoughts. What a waste of time and energy, she thought sadly. Silly daydreams and night fantasies that could end abruptly, as soon as tomorrow night. Once they lured Shore and everything went as planned, she and Leslie would be on a return flight to Wisconsin. There'd be no cozy fires, no laughter shared by lovers, and certainly no tomorrows beyond the task ahead of them.

Concentrate on the job ahead, she chastised herself. *Think about finding Leslie.*

She drew in a deep breath. "O'Neill?"

"Yeah?"

"Where do the copper wires go?"

She saw him attempt to smother a grin, and fail. "They, uh, circle the underside of your breasts."

Heat crept into her cheeks and she was grateful she'd asked him to not turn on the light. "Like an underwire bra?"

"Uh-huh."

He pushed off the leather chair and stood. "You should try and get some sleep. G'night, Bailey."

"O'Neill?" she called.

He stopped and looked over his shoulder at her. "Yeah?"

"I am sorry I didn't tell you sooner. I mean, before you...before we..."

"It's okay, Bailey."

"Are you sure?"

"Yeah. Forget about it," he said, then disappeared down the hall.

Forget about it?

She'd never forget what she'd done with O'Neill. She'd never forget those moments in his arms when he'd made her feel alive, special.

Forget about it?

"Impossible," she whispered to no one but the darkness. To do so would be to forget O'Neill.

And he was forever imprinted on her heart and soul.

9

THE SETTING OF THE SUN brought no reprieve from the soaring temperatures to the streets of Los Angeles. Not so much as a breeze from the ocean made its way along Hollywood Boulevard. The people who made their living on the streets, a few legally, and too many to count illegally, had left their hiding places to ply their trade in the sultry night, hoping to make a quick buck that would get them through to the next night.

The inside of the surveillance van was hot, stuffy and nearly unbearable. Mason's shirt clung to his back, his jeans felt glued to his legs. He wiped the sweat from his forehead and lifted the binoculars, zeroing in on Bailey standing near an unused mail drop less than fifty yards from Shadee's. They'd dressed her in the same outrageous, gaudy outfit she'd worn the night he'd dragged her into the station, sans the dark wig. With the garter belt, lace leggings and thigh-high boots, she looked overdone but not too far out of place amid the seasoned hookers, street bums and the few tourists foolish enough to venture onto Hollywood Boulevard after dark. Provided he made an appearance, Shore would spot her. Hell, he couldn't miss her.

"Talk to me, Bailey," Mason muttered, although she couldn't hear him. They'd opted for a one-way communication system. If they'd chosen a two-way, there was a greater chance of Shore discovering the wire when, or if, Bailey went away with him.

Just the thought of Bailey near Shore tightened his neck and shoulders with tension. A ball of acid churned in his stomach. God, if anything happened to her... No, he couldn't allow his thoughts to wander down that road. But still, he worried, and he'd taken every extra precaution he could to make certain she wouldn't be alone on the streets tonight.

Mason adjusted the headset, moving the microphone closer. "Crandall, anything on your end?" he asked into the mouthpiece.

"Nothing since you asked me five minutes ago," Crandall muttered.

Mason scanned the street with the binoculars and found Crandall. The undercover officer sat on the dirty sidewalk outside of Shadee's, his legs pulled up to his chest and his head resting against his crossed arms. He looked like a street bum catching a few winks. "Just keep your eyes open," Mason ordered.

They'd been in the van for four hours, and nothing. Not a sign of Shore or any of his cronies. Another hour and they'd have to call it a night. If Shore hadn't materialized by 1:00 a.m., chances were pretty slim that he'd be showing his face tonight.

"Damn, it's hot in here," Blake complained. "Why the hell couldn't we have set up in the motel across the street, where there's air-conditioning?"

Mason scanned the street looking for the other undercover officers. He found Kate Morgan, sashaying across the road toward Bailey, wearing a short white skirt, a hot-pink halter top and spiked heels of the same shade. She strolled to the bus stop and sat, waving with enthusiasm to a convertible filled with teenage boys shouting propositions as they drove past.

"Because if Shore gets near Bailey, I want to be able to move in quickly," he said, scanning farther down the street to John Reynolds. Reynolds, dressed as a street punk, moved along the sidewalk on a skateboard.

"You've got three people on her, they're not going to let her out of their sight," Blake reasoned, then reached for the cooler filled with ice-cold bottles of water. He twisted off the top, then drained the bottle in one try.

"I'm not willing to take that risk."

Blake blew out a breath filled with frustration, then readjusted his headset. "Kate, get that adorable behind of yours up and moving, sweetheart."

"Bite me, Hammond," she said. "My feet are killing me and I'm suffocating under this damn wig."

"Then go barefoot," Mason barked into the microphone. "Get moving."

"Hey, take it easy, partner." Blake smothered a grin when he spotted Kate flipping them the bird. "We've been out here for four hours and we haven't seen a thing yet. It's Sunday. Business is bound to be a little slow tonight."

"She's moving," Mason said, and his body tensed. "Bailey's moving." He kept the binoculars on her. She pushed away from the mailbox and walked slowly along the boulevard, closer to Shadee's.

She stopped outside the club.

"Dammit, what is she doing? She's coming toward you, Crandall."

"I see her," Crandall muttered, then slowly, as if every movement cost him, he stood, using the wall to support him.

Bailey edged closer to Shadee's and peered inside. She glanced at Crandall, then dismissed him. Mason had told her there were three officers on the streets who'd be watching, but he hadn't told her who they were, just that they'd be close by as a safeguard.

She looked over her shoulder, toward the van, then stepped inside the blues joint.

Mason threw his headset on the floorboard, swearing a blue streak. He reached for the door handle, intent on going after her and dragging her back to the safe house, where she'd stay until they found Shore and her sister.

Blake put a hand on his shoulder. "Wait a minute, Mason."

"Like hell." He jerked on the handle.

"We can hear her," Blake said in a reasonable tone. "We'll know if she's approached. You go charging after her now, you're going to blow the whole operation."

"They'll think she's under my protection," he argued.

"Exactly. And we need Shore to believe she's in *need* of protection and has no ties."

Mason knew his partner was right, but he didn't like it. If Shore believed Bailey was operating solo, the chances of him offering his protection were higher. Dammit, he didn't like it, not one bit. History was close to making a repeat performance. Using a civilian was bad news, and Bailey was no exception. He'd been hesitant all along about using her, but now that he knew how truly innocent she was, he was close to admitting he was afraid, especially if they managed to get her inside and Shore discovered she was a plant.

"I'll send Kate in to keep an eye on her," Blake said. He crawled back to the surveillance equipment to issue the instructions to the female undercover officer.

After a moment, Mason followed. He slipped on the headset and heard the haunting rhythm of the blues through the earphones. Picking up the binoculars again, he kept his gaze on the entrance to Shadee's.

And waited.

BLUE SMOKE CURLED around her. The stench of cheap alcohol, unwashed bodies and cloying perfume assailed her senses. In the corner on a raised dais, a four-piece band played while a heavyset woman in a black sequined dress a size too small belted out classic Billie Holiday in the most beautiful voice Bailey had ever heard.

She scanned the crowd. Men, and a few women, were seated at a long bar, some in animated conversation, others with their heads down staring into their drinks, giving off signals that said to leave them alone. Around the perimeter of the room were small round tables filled with patrons, their demeanor much the same as their counterparts at the bar. She sensed a hopelessness among the quiet ones, and an almost desperate need to forget.

She didn't know why she'd walked into Shadee's, maybe because she hoped she'd find Shore, but now that she was here she realized she'd been wrong. From the things that Blake and O'Neill had told her about the man, he wasn't the type to slink through the back door of any establishment. Looking around at the shabby interior and even shabbier patrons, she found it difficult to imagine someone as polished as Shore patronizing the run-down blues club.

She found an empty seat at the bar and climbed up on the stool. The bartender, a grisly-looking fellow with biceps rivaling a side of beef, stared her down. She offered him a weak grin when he approached.

"What'll it be?" Grisly asked, his voice as rough as the rest of him.

She wasn't much of a drinker, and generally ordered white wine the times she'd been asked to attend a business dinner with a new client. Any of the other drinks she'd tried whenever she'd gone out with the girls were frothy and female. Grisly didn't look too adept at mixing Chi-Chi's or Blue Hawaii's, and she seriously doubted blender operation in a place like this. From the looks of the crowd, those who frequented Shadee's came in for one purpose, to get drunk and get there fast.

"Well?" Grisly asked again, his scowl deepening. "I ain't got all night, girlie."

"Tequila, straight up," she said, hoping to convey a modicum of authority on the subject.

Grisly grunted, then slapped a napkin on the bar in front of her. He followed up with a short glass that looked clean in spite of its surroundings, then filled it with golden elixir guaranteed to make the imbiber forget their woes for a brief period of time. A saltshaker and a quarter section of a not-very-fresh-looking lime followed.

She gave a weak grin of thanks, pulled the glass closer to her and waited, for what she wasn't quite sure.

"TEQUILA?" Blake shook his head. "I never would have guessed her for a Cuervo girl."

Mason said nothing. He was seething, and didn't trust his voice to not betray his feelings. All the years he'd been a cop, he'd never allowed his emotions to interfere with the job. Even the night the sting had gone bad and Jim and Ashley had been murdered by Shore, he'd kept it together.

Until now.

Until one petite blonde, with cornflower blue eyes and a body that could drive a man to his knees with need, tripped into his life and turned him inside out.

He scowled. When he got his hands on her, he was going to read her the riot act. Of all the stupid, asinine—

"Mason, look."

Mason shifted his gaze. A sleek gunmetal gray Mercedes, with dark tinted windows, pulled in front of Shadee's. Mason tensed.

Shore.

The door opened and a tall woman with rich cocoa skin wearing a short, black spandex dress stepped from the car. She slammed the door closed, then strode into the blues club.

On the earphones, he heard a sharp gasp from Bailey.

BAILEY RECOGNIZED her the moment the woman stepped into the club. The same woman Shore had threatened at knifepoint two evenings before. She wore black with lots of gold chains wrapped around the slender column of her throat. The dress covered the essentials, but not much more.

The woman stepped up to the bar beside Bailey and called out for the bartender to bring her a bourbon and water.

Bailey bit her lip. This woman was connected to Devlin Shore. Whether or not she worked for him, she didn't know, but there was only one way to find out. Ask.

She turned her attention to the woman. She sucked in a sharp breath at the dark bruise covering her left eye.

The woman looked down at her, her dark soulful eyes filled with mistrust. "What are you lookin' at?"

"I'm sorry. That must hurt," she said, indicating the bruise.

"What's it to you?"

She had a dialogue going. Hostile, but the woman was talking to her, at least.

"Some john get a little rough with you, eh?"

The woman made a sound, close to a laugh, but Bailey couldn't be certain.

"It's getting harder and harder to make a living," Bailey improvised. "And more dangerous."

The woman reached into a small sequined bag and produced a pack of cigarettes. She shook one out of the pack and lit it, inhaling deeply. "Yeah, well, things are tough all over, kid. Hey," she called to the bartender. "You send away to Kentucky for that bourbon or what?"

"Yeah, yeah, in a minute, Roxanne."

"I've been thinking about maybe finding some protection," Bailey said. "You know, someone to screen the clients first. I've been stiffed for money twice this week already."

Roxanne leaned against the bar and faced Bailey. "You a working girl?"

"Sure," Bailey said with a shrug. "Aren't you?"

"Yeah, you could say that," Roxanne answered cryptically. Grisly delivered Roxanne's drink, then disappeared to the opposite end of the bar. Roxanne brought the glass to her lips, and eyed Bailey over the rim. "You looking for a pimp?"

The lady stopped singing the blues, but no one clapped in appreciation. Sadly, she began another song, this one more mournful than the last.

Bailey reached for her drink and brought it to her lips. The sharp, tangy liquid burned its way down her throat and settled into her belly like a ball of fire. Good gracious, that was strong stuff.

She set the glass aside and looked at Roxanne. The woman had probably been beautiful once. Now she just looked old and distrustful. "I think it'd be safer, don't you?"

Roxanne tossed back her bourbon and water, then called Grisly for another drink. "What's a kid like you doing turning tricks anyway? Shouldn't you be in college somewhere?"

Bailey shrugged. "Everyone's gotta make a living."

Grisly delivered another drink to Roxanne. She toyed with her glass for a minute, then looked at Bailey again, her expression thoughtful. "I know someone who might be interested in representing you."

Representing her? Jeez-oh-Pete, the woman made it sound so businesslike and aboveboard. "I'm listening."

Roxanne straightened. She narrowed her eyes and ran her gaze over Bailey before taking another sip from her drink. "You be here tomorrow night," Roxanne said. "If he likes what he sees, he'll be in touch."

Roxanne pushed away from the bar and disappeared down a long corridor. Bailey resisted the urge to follow. What if Roxanne was going to see Shore right now? Instead, she slipped off the bar stool and headed for the front door, confident that they'd at least made some progress. What had been a long boring night had turned into a lead, and brought her that much closer to finding her sister.

She walked outside into the warmth of the evening. Casually, she strolled down the street to the car that would be waiting for her two blocks away.

"In case you didn't hear all that, O'Neill," she said quietly as she turned the corner, "tomorrow night we meet Devlin Shore."

SHE SAT QUIETLY as the undercover officer who'd introduced himself as John Reynolds drove through the streets of Los Angeles to the pre-arranged meeting place. She didn't see why he couldn't just take her to the safe house, but O'Neill was being overly cautious. Only himself, Detective Hammond and Lieutenant Forbes knew the location of the safe house, and he planned to keep it that way.

"Good work, Ms. Grayson," Detective Reynolds said as he pulled into the parking lot of a shopping center. Reynolds looked young, but the ID he'd showed her when he climbed into the car had indicated he was over twenty-eight. He didn't look a day over nineteen, and the skateboard in the back seat did little to refute that assumption.

"Thank you," she said. "I think we got lucky."

Reynolds pulled alongside Mason's truck then put the car in park. "How'd you know about Roxanne?" he asked, turning off the headlights. He kept the engine idling, and the cool air-conditioning washed over her.

"I saw her with Shore a couple of nights ago." She remembered the flash of the knife Shore had waved at Roxanne, and shuddered. Tomorrow night she'd meet the man who had her sister. The man who'd killed William Greene. The man who sold countless young and desperate women.

She prayed she wouldn't make any mistakes.

The white surveillance van pulled into the parking lot. Detective Hammond guided the van next to the idling car where she waited with Detective Reynolds. The door opened and O'Neill stepped from the vehicle, slamming the door with enough force to make her jump.

O'Neill strode toward her. Sweet heaven, he was angry. She had the wild urge to lock the doors and instruct Reynolds to drive away.

His face could have been made from stone, and as he neared, she saw that his eyes glittered dangerously. He was more than angry. He was livid.

He opened her door and she half expected him either to pull her roughly from the vehicle or start yelling at her. He did neither. He held the door and waited for her to exit the car. When she did, he slammed that door, as well.

"O'Neill, I can—"

"Save it," he said, his voice as hard as the expression on his face.

"But—"

"Not now," he said tightly, unlocking the door to the truck. He waited for her to slip inside, then shut the door and left to say something to Reynolds.

By the time he returned to the Bronco, Bailey's nerves were stretched tight. She'd suspected he might be angry with her when she'd slipped out of sight for a while, but she had not been prepared for the fury radiating from him or the coldness of his expression.

Without a word, he started the truck, then pulled out of the parking lot. Silently, he drove over the city streets to the freeway, then took the exit that would lead them back to the safe house in the hills. A quick glance in his direction revealed his temper hadn't cooled. The dash lights cast his face in shadows, but she had no trouble detecting the tightened jaw and the dangerous gleam in his eyes.

She hoped by the time they pulled up to the gates of the safe house, he'd have calmed down. Her hopes sank when he gunned the engine and they sped up the driveway to the house. When he slammed the door to the vehicle with enough force to rattle the windows, her hopes completely dissolved.

He rounded the truck with long strides and headed straight for the front door, not even stopping to open her door for her as he'd done since she'd met him. With a deep sigh, she followed him. He unlocked the front door and pushed it open. She expected him to storm into the house, instead, he waited for her to precede him.

Keeping her gaze averted, and with a great deal of reluctance, she stepped past him. She walked into the living room and turned on a lamp. For a moment, she considered going to her room to wait until he calmed down, but she'd never been one to run away from a confrontation, and she wasn't about to start now. She sat down on the sofa and waited.

He closed the door, quietly this time, and strode through the living room to the kitchen area. She heard him open the door to Jo's crate, followed by the sounds of him preparing bowls of food and water for the dog.

An eternity passed before she heard the sliding glass door open when O'Neill let Jo out for her nightly romp around the grounds. Bailey looked up as he came into the living room. The hardness in his eyes hadn't dissipated, and a muscle in his jaw twitched, she imagined, because he was busy grinding his teeth in frustrated anger.

He glared at her.

She lifted her chin and glared right back.

He crossed his arms over his chest and braced his feet apart. "Do you want to tell me what the hell you think you were doing out there tonight, before I take you to the airport?" He kept his voice low and measured, controlled, she thought.

"Airport?"

"That's right. Playtime is over, Bailey. You're going home."

10

BAILEY SHOT OFF the sofa. "You can't make me leave."

"The hell I can't," Mason roared. "You're out of here, Bailey. Tonight."

Before she could blink, he grabbed her wrist and started down the hallway toward the bedrooms. "You risked your neck," he said, pushing open her door and pulling her inside. "You risked the lives of officers."

He left her near the bed, turned on the lamp, then stormed across the room to the closet. He yanked open the door, pulled out her gym bag and slammed it on the dresser. "You were supposed to remain in plain sight where we could all keep an eye on you and make sure you were safe."

He dragged open the drawers on the dresser, scooped up some of her things and shoved them into the gym bag.

"Mason, please—"

He faced her, his eyebrows lowered in a furious scowl above his chilling gaze. "What the hell were you thinking?" he shouted.

She shoved her hands into the back pockets of her denim shorts. "I was attempting to initiate contact. We know Shore frequents Shadee's. I thought he might have used the back entrance."

He swore a blue streak. "It wasn't your job to *initiate contact*. You were to wait until Shore approached you. Period!"

A jolt of anger went through her. "I stood out there on that street for four hours," she retorted heatedly. "Other than a few sleazy propositions, we had nothing. You should be thanking me."

"Thanking you?" He laughed, but the sound held no humor, only the deep dark anger brewing inside him. "Thanking you," he repeated. "You took an unnecessary risk."

"I walked into a bar, O'Neill. It's not like I had a sign pasted to my back that said Police Plant," she snapped, her voice dripping with sarcasm.

He moved quickly toward her. She had the good sense to back away, sensing that control he tried so hard to keep a lid on was about to slip.

Her back brushed against the wall. When she looked into his eyes, the coldness there chilled her, effectively defusing her burst of anger. This was not the O'Neill she knew and trusted. This O'Neill frightened her.

"What you did was foolish." His tone was even again, controlled, but still seething with unleashed fury. The control gave her little comfort, nor did his claim.

Yes, she admitted silently, she had acted foolishly. Since she'd gotten involved with O'Neill, she'd repeatedly argued that she would keep her head, she wouldn't take unnecessary risks. And what had she done? Exactly what he'd told her she'd do since they'd started working together.

"All I did was have a drink inside the club. I

didn't know Roxanne was going to show up," she explained in an attempt to placate him.

His gaze narrowed. "You remembered her from Friday night, didn't you?"

"It's hard to forget seeing Shore wave that knife in her face. Anyway, I wasn't sure, but I took a guess and figured she might be working for him."

"Oh, she works for him, all right," O'Neill said. He planted his hands on his hips and gave her a level look. "We have a line on her and have been watching her for some time. She runs one of Shore's 'escort services.' We don't know for certain, but we think she could be the link to the sales. She's got the connections to make them happen."

"Oh my God," she whispered. Something that had been bothering her for the past day clicked into place, something that hadn't quite made sense to her, until now. If William Greene had been killed because he'd gotten too close, then Shore was indeed planning to sell Leslie. Greene must have learned about the slavery ring. What other discovery would have necessitated his murder? And if what Mason said was true, Roxanne more than likely knew where Leslie was being held.

The rationalization made her more determined than ever to continue with the sting as planned. And she would. With or without O'Neill's help.

"If Roxanne is the one arranging the sales, then it's a good thing I did talk to her."

He reached for her, taking hold of her arms. She struggled, but he tightened his grip. "What you did tonight was incredibly stupid. You took an unnecessary risk. Your part in this is over."

"No, Mason," she said, shrugging out of his

grasp. "I'm *not* leaving. I'm going back tomorrow and I'm going to finish this."

"Forget it, Bailey." He strode across the room and began throwing more of her clothes into the gym bag.

Fine, let him send her packing, she thought. He could take her to the airport and even put her on the plane, but when it took off, she'd be on the ground and headed right back to Hollywood Boulevard to await Devlin Shore. She hadn't come this far to turn tail and run now.

But first, she had to at least try to make Mason listen to reason. He needed her. She was his way into Shore's dirty world. For him to throw it all away when they were so close made little sense.

She dropped onto the edge of the bed, watching as he continued to shove her clothes into the bag. "Mason, listen to me," she said, fighting to keep her tone reasonable. She didn't need him to find Leslie, but it sure made her feel a heck of a lot safer knowing he was there in case things turned ugly. "We're close. You can't call an end to this now."

"If you're worried about your sister, don't be," he said, opening another drawer. "I'll find her."

"I've already made contact," she argued. "Roxanne said she'd send Shore to see me tomorrow. If he likes what he sees, then I'm in. Don't blow this now."

"You're out of it!"

"Dammit, O'Neill," she snapped in frustration. She shot off the bed and snatched the gym bag from him. "Are you even listening to me? We're close, I tell you. Damn close. I could be in tomorrow."

He took the bag from her, zipped it up and set it near the door. "Forget it, Bailey. It's not going to happen," he said, then stalked out of the room.

She followed him, fixed on making him see reason.

She grabbed his arm in an attempt to stop him. "Why?" she demanded.

He shrugged her off and lengthened his stride. "I said to forget it," he said coldly, not even looking at her.

She trotted after him, following him into the kitchen. "Why, O'Neill? Does being in control mean that much to you that you'd pitch what we've accomplished into the wind?"

He stopped for a brief second, then moved over to the phone. Obviously she'd hit a nerve.

He punched a series of numbers into the keypad, ignoring her taunt. The man had to be made of stone. And she was getting desperate.

"What are you so afraid of?" she shouted.

He slammed the phone on the hook and spun around to face her. His eyes blazed with fury, but she held her ground.

"You want the truth?" he asked, his voice vibrating with anger. "I've been here before, Bailey. I've used a plant hoping to bring Shore out into the open. I gambled and two people paid with their lives. I'm not going to allow you to get yourself killed. If you don't have the good sense to do as you're told, then you're not going out there again."

He turned his back on her and stared out the sliding glass door into the darkness of the night. He lifted his hand to rub at the back of his neck.

Understanding dawned, and her heart went out

to him. Slowly, she crossed the space separating them. She wanted to comfort him, but fear of being rejected kept her from wrapping her arms around him and holding him close. "Who were they to you?" she asked quietly.

For the longest time he simply continued to stare into the darkness. She didn't think he was going to answer. Finally, he said, "My partner, and a young woman."

"I'm sorry, Mason," she whispered, knowing her words were paltry comfort. She hadn't been wrong in her assumption that Mason was a very caring man. The obvious pain he felt at the loss of his partner and a civilian plant touched her deep inside.

He took hold of her hand before opening the sliding glass door. She followed him into the night, where only the buzzing of mosquitoes and a serenade of crickets interrupted the solitude. He led them to the low brick retaining wall and sat. Keeping her hand clasped within his, he waited for her to sit beside him.

He let out a long breath, then looked down at her. "Jim Evers and I were in the SEALs together. After I left the service, we lost touch for a while. I had no idea he lived in L.A. Not long after Karen's transfer, I made detective. They transferred me to another station, and Jim and I became partners. He'd been investigating a homicide involving Devlin Shore and getting nowhere until we found a link.

"That link was a witness, Ashley Adams. She'd been busted on a solicitation charge. Jim wanted Shore bad, so I laid some pretty heavy-duty pressure on her. I told her if she didn't agree to help us, she'd more than likely go to prison. The kid was scared, but we wanted the collar on Shore. Rather than face a prison sentence, she agreed to help us."

So Mason *had* played "bad cop" before. After his tirade earlier, it didn't take much of a stretch of the imagination to understand he'd be good at that part of the job. Because he'd played the heavy and coerced a witness into a series of events that led to her death, and that of his partner, he was plagued with guilt. Guilt she understood. It had been her constant companion since Leslie disappeared.

"How was she linked to Shore?"

"She was a small-time operator, turning tricks occasionally. She wasn't a bad person. She didn't deal drugs, she wasn't a user. The kid was alone in the world trying to make ends meet. The only mistake she made was taking the easy route by hooking up with Shore for protection. Then one day, she saw too much...."

"Somehow I don't get the impression prostitution is exactly an easy profession," she said with a gentle smile. "What happened?"

"We set up a sting and it went sour," he said quietly. "Someone on the inside tipped Shore off, but we never uncovered the snitch. Jim and Ashley were both killed. The bitch of it is, we never had enough on Ashley to send her to prison. The D.A. would have let her walk without even pressing charges, but she didn't know that, and we didn't tell her. We used her."

She finally understood his pain, and the demons that rode him so hard. She also understood the reasons he fought her, pushed her and bullied her into doing things his way.

"Mason, this is different. You're not using me."

"Maybe not, but I don't want to see anything happen to you. When you walked into that nightclub, I just about came unglued. You're bad news for me, Bailey."

"You saying you care, O'Neill?" she teased, trying not to read too much into his words.

He grew quiet again and stood. She wished she knew what he was thinking, what else he was afraid to tell her. O'Neill didn't open himself up to others easily, she could see that. And it didn't take a rocket scientist to figure out what he'd just shared with her wasn't something he spoke of often.

He tugged on her hand, guiding her until she stood in front of him. Gently, he placed his hands on her hips and drew her near. Her breath caught and a delicious warmth curled around the sudden ache growing inside her.

"I do care," he murmured, "and that makes you dangerous."

She lifted her arms and wreathed them around his neck, closing the remaining distance between them. She breathed in the warm, male scent of him and her senses spiked, along with the soaring of her heart.

His gaze dropped to her lips and she shivered.

"Kiss me, Mason," she whispered, then brought their mouths together tentatively.

What she'd hoped would be a kiss to offer comfort, quickly turned into something more, something needy that took her by surprise. He quickly pressed his advantage, slanting his mouth over hers. Pulling her tighter against him, he crushed her body to his, holding her as if he feared she'd escape. She reveled in the sensations ribboning through her, the way her breasts pressed against his wide chest, the erotic promise of his searching mouth. There was magic between them, and no matter how much O'Neill tried to deny their attraction, one thing was clear: they wanted each other. The only question was whether or not they'd go further than deep kisses and bone-melting caresses.

For her, there was only one acceptable answer.

He ended the kiss long before she was ready to let him go. Tomorrow night the chances were high that she'd meet up with their quarry. Mason had told her countless times that things go wrong, not every move can be calculated because of variables. No matter how well planned, there was always the possibility she could end up just like Ashley Adams, or heaven forbid, something could happen to Mason.

She looked at him, at the need and desire in his intense amber gaze, and knew what she had to do.

"Come with me," she said.

He followed her into the house and down the corridor to her bedroom. Kicking her gym bag aside, she stepped into the room and urged him to sit on the edge of the bed. "Wait here. I want to look like me, not some dime-store floozy, when you hear what I have to say."

After he nodded in agreement, she snagged her gym bag and headed into the bathroom. She closed the door, stripped off her tacky-wear, carefully removing the wire and setting it on the counter before stepping beneath the hot spray of the shower. She washed her hair, scrubbed the thick layers of makeup from her face, then washed the smoke and grit from her skin.

Wrapping her hair in a towel, she stepped from the shower and dried herself with another huge fluffy towel, feeling more like herself. O'Neill would try to deny her. Tell her he was protecting her. That was his nature, and part of what she loved about him. He had a need to protect those around him, and it endeared him in her heart. But this time she'd make him see reason. This time she'd make him understand her point of view.

Digging through her gym bag, she located her nightgown and slipped it over her head. By the time she'd brushed her hair free of tangles, twenty minutes had passed. Gathering her courage she stepped from the bathroom.

O'Neill remained on the bed, where she'd left him. He was leaning forward, his elbows braced on his knees, his hands clasped in front of him. When he looked at her, she detected a hint of wariness in his gaze.

She approached him, gently reaching out to run her hand along his cheek. He grasped her wrist before she touched him. "What do you want, Bailey?"

You, she nearly said, but kept the thought, and the truth, to herself for the moment. There'd be time later for revelations.

She sat on the bed beside him, and he released her. "Tell me what will happen tomorrow, Mason."

He looked at her with a softness in his eyes that altered his usually forbidding look. It gave her hope.

"Am I getting on a plane back to Wisconsin, or am I going to meet Shore?"

He blew out a sigh and stood. He walked to the window, braced his arm on the wooden frame and said nothing. Little skitters of unease eddied down her spine. He could refuse to allow her to return to the streets, but he probably knew she'd show up anyway and be waiting outside of Shadee's. More than likely, O'Neill would arrest her, this time charging her with obstruction of justice or impeding an investigation or some other excuse just to get her out of the path of danger. That was O'Neill. That was his way.

Or they could do this her way, and save them both a lot of frustration.

She scooted to the center of the bed. Pulling her knees to her chest, she adjusted her nightgown, then wrapped her arms around her legs and watched him.

"I know what you're thinking, O'Neill," she said when he remained silent. "You're weighing the consequences of putting another civilian in Shore's path. Am I going to end up like Ashley Adams? Or will it work this time and you'll finally avenge your partner's and Ashley's deaths by bringing Shore to justice?"

"You think you know me so well," he said, looking over his shoulder at her. "What do *you* think I'm going to do?"

"I don't know, Mason. You want Shore, but at what cost this time? But this time it isn't the same. I'm here willingly. I'm not some poor frightened young girl who'll do just about anything so I won't have to face a prison sentence. I'm here because I'm convinced Shore has my sister. If we continue the sting, I'm here of my own free will."

"Bull." The frown was back, along with anger in his eyes. "Don't give me that, lady. You're willing to put your life on the line because of some misplaced sense of loyalty. You save your sister, you absolve your own guilt."

She shrugged. "Doesn't make us all that much different, does it, O'Neill?"

"You're wrong," he said heatedly.

"Am I? You're putting your life on the line because of some misplaced sense of loyalty to the memory of your partner and a girl the two of you coerced. I fail to see the difference. Loyalty is loyalty, Mason, no matter which way you slice it."

He just glared at her, but she saw the war in his eyes, the fight between wanting Shore and wanting to keep her safe. "I don't want you there."

"Why?" she pressed. "You *were* willing to use me. Why the sudden change of heart?"

He turned his gaze back to the window. "Because I care what happens to you."

"And you didn't care about Ashley Adams, did you? That's the difference, isn't it, Mason?"

He shoved away from the window and faced her. "No, dammit, I didn't. Not until it was too late. Is that what you want to hear?" he asked, his voice heavy with self-loathing. "You want to hear that I was a cold-blooded bastard no better than Shore?"

"You're not like him," she said gently, scooting off the bed to approach him. She reached up and brushed a fallen lock of hair from his forehead, smoothing it back in place. Her hand trailed from his hair to his chest, where she rested it over the beating of his heart.

"You're blaming yourself, carrying this around inside you, and that's so wrong. You had no idea that things were going to turn out the way they did. How many times have you told me, there are variables in every situation and you have to be ready to switch gears to compensate? You're a good cop, Mason. And you're a good man."

His eyes narrowed with annoyance, but he didn't push her away, or offer a rebuttal to her impassioned speech.

"Tomorrow night I'm going back to Shadee's to meet Shore," she told him. "If he makes me an offer, I'm going to go away with him just like we planned. You and Blake and who knows how many other undercover officers will be close behind. I'll be in a dangerous situation, and it's possible something could go wrong. But it's my choice, Mason. No matter what happens, I want you to know that I'm doing this knowing the risks."

The muscle in his jaw clenched. "All right, Bailey," he said suddenly. "You win. But you do it my way, and if you so much as deviate one iota, I'm calling it off. Is that clear?"

She offered him a weak grin. "As crystal. But one more thing."

He let out a long sigh. "What now?"

Her courage wavered. This was it, her one chance and she didn't know if she could go through with her own plan of action.

Before she completely chickened out, she pulled in a deep breath.

"I want you to make love to me," she blurted out, then flicked off the lamp.

11

THE EFFECT of her sweet command was instantaneous and demanding. A powerful wave of longing gripped Mason's gut and wouldn't let go. He didn't know what surprised him more, her request or his response.

Moonlight bathed the room in a white glow, illuminating her. Her perfect body was silhouetted beneath the sheer fabric of the nightgown he'd barely noticed before. He shook his head and took a step back. "Wait a minute, Bailey—"

"Hear me out." The pleading note in her voice combined with steely determination stopped him cold. In all his life, in all his years on the force, if he'd learned anything, it was the certainty that there was nothing more dangerous than a determined woman. He was in trouble, but not exactly looking for a savior.

"If I end up going with Shore tomorrow night, we don't really know what could happen. If he discovers the wire, he could kill me on the spot."

Icy fear crept up his spine at the truth of her words. "Bailey, don't…" He couldn't bear the thought of losing her. When their time together ended, they'd go their separate ways, but he didn't want to think about losing her to violence. Especially the brand Shore specialized in handing out to those who got in his way.

"Or, he could... Well, you said yourself I'd be lucky if all he did was kill me...." She stepped closer, laying her hand on his arm. Her touch was light and gentle, and as sweet as anything he'd ever felt.

He lifted an eyebrow and looked down at her. "So I'm the lesser of two evils, is that it?"

She smiled at his attempt at levity. "No," she said, with a gentle shake of her head. "I want my first time to be special, with someone I care about. I don't want to look back years from now and think about how horrible it was. I want wonderful memories to carry with me, not haunting nightmares."

He backed away from her, lifting his hands as if she held a gun to his chest. She was asking for too much. They had no future together, and her bravado wasn't reason enough for a one-night stand. She deserved more, much more than he could give her. Happiness was what she deserved, and he had nothing to offer her but disappointment. "Bailey, look, I don't—"

She advanced, and he took another step back, his rear coming in contact with the thick pine bedpost. "I want *you*, Mason."

Slowly, she lifted her hands and began unfastening the buttons of his shirt. "And I know you want me." Her voice was tinged with sex and sin, and having a strong effect on his resistance.

She yanked the shirt free of his jeans, then splayed her palms over his chest. "What's wrong with two people caring about each other sharing something so beautiful?"

His muscles flexed beneath her touch, and his body responded to her plea, hardening to the point of pain.

"Make love to me, Mason," she whispered, pressing her lips to his chest. "Make a beautiful memory with me."

A sound, somewhere between a moan of pain and a growl, ripped from his throat. How could he deny her? God, he wanted her.

Her tongue snaked out and laved at his nipple, sending another flash of heat spiraling south. Gripping her shoulders, he set her from him, unable to bear her sensuous brand of torture another moment. "There'll be no turning back after we make love," he managed to say.

Emotion filled her eyes as she looked up at him. He detected no fear, no hesitation, only complete trust, open and pure. She held his gaze, she held him mesmerized. "I know," she whispered, then lifted her gown over her head.

His mouth went dry. "We shouldn't do this," he said hoarsely, his fingers itching to touch her, his body craving hers. The need to possess her, to mate, to make her his was overwhelming.

"But we will," she said, wreathing her arms around his neck and pressing her slender body to his.

He was fighting a losing battle, and threw out the white flag in surrender. Unable to stop himself, he captured her lips in a hard, possessive kiss, tasting her sweetness. He needed his head examined, but he couldn't deny her, or his own need, a moment longer.

Carefully, he guided her onto the bed and its soft

comforter, surrounding her with his body. She moaned, the sound as warm and intimate as the sweet, fresh scent that was hers alone. The part of him he'd fought to keep closed off from her shattered. In spite of his attempts to remain emotionally removed, he could no longer deny he wanted her as he hadn't wanted another woman in a very long time.

Tonight, there would be no turning back. Tonight, all night, she would be his. He'd deal with tomorrow later.

Her hands slipped beneath his shirt in tentative exploration, and he suffered the sweet agony of her touch. He knew he should stop before they reached the point of no return. She deserved more than what he could offer her, which was nothing but the memories she'd practically begged him to create with her. But she drew him in and held him spellbound, erasing his common sense, leaving only fierce desire and the strong need to possess her.

Dragging his lips from hers, he teased her with quick darting kisses along her jaw and down her throat to the gentle swell of her breasts. His hand skimmed over her hip, slowly moving over her body, imprinting every line and contour to memory.

She arched her back when his fingers brushed against her breast. He tested the full feminine weight, the soft flesh hot and silky in his hands. She wove her fingers through his hair and pulled him down, urging him to take her in his mouth. His name fell sweetly from her lips, and he was lost. The woman was going to drive him insane, and he had no choice but to love every minute of this journey.

He found heaven in her sweet embrace. Every part of his body came alive with sensation. He'd never have enough of her. She was everything that was good and pure. And whether he deserved her or not, for tonight, she was his.

Need rippled through him, not only physically, but emotionally. The realization that he more than desired Bailey, but needed her on an emotional level, should have left him cold. Instead, it fired his blood.

His control was slipping, and fast. If he didn't slow them both down, they were going to be over and done with much quicker than either of them intended. Rolling away from her, he shrugged out of his shirt. His shoes, jeans and shorts followed, landing in the same heap as her nightgown.

"I thought you were leaving me," she said, wiggling closer as he slid over her.

"Not on your life, lady," he answered, nuzzling her neck. She drew inarticulate patterns over his back and down to his buttocks, where she gently pressed her fingers into the muscle. His blood heated at her hesitant touch, the warmth fueling his desire.

He began his own sensual journey, using his tongue and fingers as he traveled over her silky curves. He moved lower, gently pressing her thighs open, teasing her with a butterfly-soft brush of his fingers against her damp curls. Her hands left his shoulders and she gripped the comforter, twisting it tightly. When he brought his mouth to her most sensitive spot, her back bowed off the bed, and his name coalesced with a moan of pure pleasure.

He gripped her hips, holding her while he continued the intimate exploration. His own blood raced hotly through his veins at her eager response.

Bailey thought she'd die from the sweet agony of his mouth pressed against her in the most intimate way a man could love a woman. Her thoughts zeroed in on the movement of his mouth combined with the intoxicating sweep of his fingers, following him blindly as he carried her dangerously close to the edge. This time, she knew what to expect, understood the craving, the need and the hot demand her body was making to the magic he created. The tension pulled her tighter, and tighter still, until she finally spun out of control, her release so powerful she cried out.

She sensed more than felt him loom above her, his hands gently smoothing her hair from her face while he whispered words of erotic promise in her ear. She opened her eyes to find passion burning in his gaze.

"Mason," she whispered as tiny tremors still racked her body. "I—"

"Shh, let me love you," he said, his voice tight with emotion. And then he kissed her, long and hard, promising her with his tongue the prophecy his body would fulfill.

Slowly, he slid his sex into her, filling her, burying himself deep inside her. She sucked in a sharp breath and slid her arms around him, holding him, trusting him to keep her safe. He thrust forward, then held himself perfectly still, giving her body time to adjust to the size and length of his. Sweat beaded on his forehead, his back coated with moisture as he waited for her pain to subside.

With a realization beyond her experience, she understood that the searing need that pulled at them both had been building from the moment he dragged her off the street to his truck. Almost from the first time he held her against those rock-hard thighs, some part of her had known that this was the man who'd steal her heart, her body and her soul. What had begun as a spark of awareness had taken a turn to something far more demanding, far more fulfilling, far more beautiful and a million times more lasting than simple lust.

Finally, the pain ebbed, and she moved against him. It was all the encouragement he needed. Slowly, he moved within her, each thrust gentle and deeper. With every stroke of his body, fire in the pit of her belly sparked, ignited, then burned hot. The heat filled her until she was powerless to do little but meet him thrust for greedy thrust as he drove her into oblivion.

When he slipped his hands beneath her bottom and thrust even more deeply, her mind slipped away and her body took control as she lost herself in his lovemaking. Liquid fire spread through her at an alarming rate, seconds before the shattering explosion that left her body racked by spasm after spasm. She clung to him, digging her nails into his strong, well-muscled back. From somewhere far away, she heard his own rough groan before he drove into her one last time.

Mason's breath came in long pants and he rested his forehead against hers, supporting himself on his elbows. "Woman," he growled, planting a hard, possessive kiss on her lips. "If you're trying to kill me, you're succeeding."

She smiled, one of those secret female smiles that told a man he was in big trouble. "Thank you, Mason."

His mouth curled into a grin. "Sweetheart, thank you is the last thing a man wants to hear after what we just did."

She giggled. "Pardon my blunder. I'm kinda new at this sort of thing."

His smile faded at her teasing reminder that he'd just taken her innocence. The primal need to mate with her had been strong, so strong he'd shucked common sense and taken what should never have belonged to him. Any attempt to console his conscience was weak at best, so he settled for the fact that Bailey was his, if only for tonight. He would let her go when their time ended. He had no other choice, and neither did she.

Carefully, he rolled off her, and tucked her against his side. She shivered when the cool air-conditioning brushed against her sweat-dampened skin, and he managed to get them beneath the blankets. "Better?" he asked around a strong craving for a cigarette.

"Hmm, much." She snuggled closer, resting her head against his shoulder, her fingers brushing at the hair on his chest.

"So if I'm not supposed to thank you, what am I supposed to say?" she asked drowsily.

He grinned when she attempted to stifle a yawn and failed. "Sleep, Bailey. That's the best compliment a woman can give a man."

"Okay," she whispered, seconds before her fingers stopped moving over his chest.

SOMETHING WOKE HIM. A sound. He listened, instantly alert. He heard it again, a low whimpering noise.

Careful not to disturb Bailey, he left the bed and slipped on his shorts. By the time he reached the sliding glass door at the rear of the house, the low whimpering had turned into a deep, pitiful howl.

"All right, old girl. I'm sorry," he said, opening the door. "I got sidetracked by a very beautiful and very demanding woman, and she exhausted me. Forgive me?"

Obviously his love life was of little interest to the dog, because Jo dashed past him into the house, her thick, bushy tail wagging happily.

The craving for a cigarette was back and sent him searching the drawers in the kitchen. Empty-handed, he blew out a long breath filled with frustration and stalked into his bedroom to continue the search, Jo on his heels.

Relief washed over him when he found an open pack on the dresser. He shook one out and felt the tension ease as he slipped the butt between his lips. A flick of the disposable lighter and he inhaled, drawing the smoke deep into his lungs.

Damn, he'd even failed at giving up smoking. With a disgusted shake of his head, he snagged the pack off the dresser and walked into the bathroom, tossing the cigarette along with the remaining pack, into the toilet.

He turned and found Jo sitting in the doorway, her black head cocked to the side. "No more," he said sternly to the dog. She wagged her tail in response, as if expressing her pride in his decision. That was Jo, he thought. Always willing to lend her support.

"Get to bed, Jo," he said, then waited for the dog to go lie beside the king-size bed before he stripped off his shorts and stepped into the shower.

He turned his back to the hot spray, then closed his eyes as images of Bailey filled his thoughts and the steaming water eased the tightened muscles in his body.

"That's one wicked grin, O'Neill."

He opened his eyes to find Bailey leaning against the opened shower door. His body responded as if her hands had touched him rather than her sultry voice. His grin deepened. "I was thinking about you."

"Hmm," she said, stepping into the shower and closing the door. Her gaze slid boldly over his body, and damn if he didn't respond like a randy eighteen-year-old schoolboy. "Looks to me like you've had some rather...uplifting thoughts."

He expected her to be shy, maybe even embarrassed or regretful after what they'd done. As much as he was enjoying her boldness, he was still surprised.

"You seem to have that effect on me," he said, reaching for her. He pulled her against him, and her soft body molded to his as if she'd been made for him. He dipped his head and nibbled on her earlobe. "Wanna have sex in the shower?"

She laughed, then wiggled against him, wrapping her arms around his waist, her hands trailing along his back in a sensuous rhythm. "Can't say that I've ever tried that before."

"The night's far from over."

She leaned back and wiggled her eyebrows at him, giving him a lascivious grin. "Promises, promises."

He chuckled, enjoying their banter more than he should. "Anyone ever tell you, you have a dirty mind?"

"No," she said. Laughing, she pressed her lips to his in a light, teasing kiss. "You're the first."

His grin faded. He didn't want to be her "first," he wanted to be her one and only. The thought of anyone knowing Bailey as intimately as he'd known her tonight made him want to commit violence. The thought spooked him. He'd never been the possessive or jealous type. Even though his marriage to Karen had failed, it hadn't been because he'd been one of those smothering husbands. In fact, quite the opposite was true. He'd never questioned her whereabouts. The few times she'd had to go out of town on business, never once had he been jealous or entertained the thought that she might be having an affair. He'd thought it had been trust, but now he wondered if perhaps complacency was the true culprit. There was no doubt in his mind that he'd loved his wife, but exactly how deep had that love gone?

Thoughts of the past flew from his mind when Bailey pressed him to one of the octagon glass walls, a wicked grin tugging her lips. "A skunk?"

"What?"

She traced the outline of the tattoo on his arm. "Your tattoo."

"I was nineteen and hammered," he said. The guys had taken him out to celebrate Cody's birth. The truth was, he'd been feeling sorry for himself because he hadn't been with Karen when his son was born. Pepe la Pew wearing a sailor's hat was just another reminder of the disappointment he'd caused the ones he'd loved.

"It's a night for discoveries," she said, trailing her tongue down his torso. "And pleasure," she added, a wicked gleam shining in her eyes before she slipped to her knees in front of him.

THE SUN RODE HIGH by the time Bailey awoke. She curled onto her side, hoping to find Mason beside her in the big four-poster bed. Disappointed, but not surprised to be alone, she dressed quickly and went in search of him.

The scents of coffee and fresh-cooked bacon drew her to the kitchen. He stood over the stove, lifting crisp bacon from a frying pan onto a paper towel–covered platter. She crept up behind him and wrapped her arms around his middle, resting her head against his broad back. "Good morning."

He moved away, effectively stepping out of her embrace. "There's coffee," he said, pulling a thick ceramic mug from the cabinet. "How many eggs do you want?"

She sighed, then poured herself some coffee. "One, thank you." Lifting the mug to her lips, she took a sip, watching him over the rim. Something had changed in the last few hours while she'd been sleeping, and she wondered if he was suddenly having regrets about the night they'd spent together.

Well, she certainly had none. She had beautiful memories of the most glorious night of her entire life with the man she loved. There'd be no turning back or pretending the night they'd shared never happened. It had, and whether he liked it or not, there *was* something between them. Something special and magical that only happened once in a lifetime.

He set the last of the bacon on the platter and carried it to the table. His lips, which had drawn out all her intimate secrets in the dark of night and early morning, were set in a grim line. If only he'd look at her, give her some hope to cling to that perhaps she wasn't the only one to have felt the magic between them, but he wouldn't. He was acting as if she wasn't even in the same room with him. Where was the man who'd tormented her with lazy sweeps of his tongue until she'd trembled in his arms? What happened to the man who'd taken her over the edge and back too many times to count throughout the night, who'd shown her the various ways of finding pleasure? What had this cold stranger done with the man she'd fallen in love with?

He finished the eggs, then carried two plates to the table. "Sit down and eat," he said, going back for buttered toast. "After breakfast we'll hit the gym for a while so you can practice what you've learned."

"Wouldn't the bedroom be more comfortable?" she quipped, referring to the other more intimate things he'd taught her.

Her attempt to lighten the mood failed, and she pulled out a chair. When he returned to the table, his expression was just as grim, and a deep frown creased his forehead.

"Not funny, huh?" She shrugged and reached for a slice of toast.

He set his mug on the table with a snap, ignoring the coffee sloshing over the sides. "If you're not going to take this seriously," he said, his voice laced with authority, "then you'll stay here tonight while we go after Shore. We don't need you now. Shore will arrive and we'll arrest him."

She dipped her toast into the soft yoke. "You have no basis for an arrest."

"I don't give a damn if I have to bust him for illegal parking," he thundered. "I'll get him into the station, and trust me, I'll find out what I need to know."

She had no doubt he could do a bang-up job. But this time he wasn't coercing some scared young girl into helping them bring down a hardened criminal. "And someone like Shore, who's been playing hide-and-seek with the cops for years, will scream for his lawyer before you get the cuffs on him. Face it, O'Neill. You need me."

The look he gave her was cold and hard, causing a shiver to chase down her spine. "I don't need you, Bailey. You've served your purpose."

Her heart constricted in her chest. His words stung, as did the coldness she'd felt from him since she'd walked into the kitchen. Anger welled inside her, and she released an impatient breath. Carefully, she set her fork on the plate and gave him a level stare. "In bed or out?"

Tension crackled between them. Her blow was intentionally low. But he'd stopped playing fair when he'd coldly rejected her, and she wasn't about to let him dismiss what they'd shared, or hide behind their purpose for working together.

He returned her stare, but there was none of the passion she'd known hidden in his gaze. Only cold, hard resolve, and something she thought might be fear. Which was ridiculous. O'Neill feared nothing.

"One has nothing to do with the other," he said with deadly calm.

She focused on the fear, and found her answer. With crystal clarity, she understood why he was so distant. A slow grin curved her lips, because she knew the truth he wasn't willing to admit even to himself.

"Oh, I think it does," she said. "You care, Mason. You care so much you'll risk your entire investigation just to keep me away from Shore. Am I that important to you that you're willing to throw away all the hours you've spent trying to nail him?"

The muscle in his jaw tightened. "Your safety—"

She stood and circled the table to stand beside him. He looked up at her and she saw the fear flash momentarily in his eyes. It gave her hope.

"No," she said, trailing her fingers along his tensed jaw. "It's more than that, but you won't admit it. You said you care. You more than care, Mason. I know it."

He pulled away from her, turning his attention to his now-cold breakfast. "You're looking for fairy tales," he said, picking up his fork. "I told you before, I'm no prince."

She smiled, a secret feminine smile that would have set his teeth on edge if he'd been watching her. "No, Mason, you're not a prince," she said quietly. "You're a just man. The man I've fallen in love with."

She walked away, leaving him alone to digest the truth along with his breakfast.

12

TWILIGHT DUSTED the spectacular view of the City
of Angels, while a cool ocean breeze chased away
the brutal heat of the summer day. Mason leaned
back into the cushioned patio chair, no closer to admitting the truth of his feelings for Bailey than he'd
been that morning.

He cared about her, worried about what could
happen to her in the next few hours when they returned to Shadee's and she came face-to-face with
Shore. But love?

Love meant tomorrows, and the truth was, they
might not have any tomorrows. He'd been a cop
long enough, had seen enough, and had more than
enough experience to know that not every plan
was executed with perfect precision. Mistakes were
made, and one wrong move could turn a solid plan
into a nightmare with fatal results.

What will you do if something happens to her?

The dreaded thought had been niggling at his
conscience for the past twenty-four hours. Now
that it had been clearly voiced, he didn't want to
think about the answer, or more, what the answer
meant to him. There was no doubt whatsoever in
his mind that he didn't want Bailey harmed. Just
the thought of her out of his sight for more than a
minute drove him crazy. Tonight, she'd be more

than out of his sight, she'd be with Shore. And that scared the hell out of him.

If all went well, in a couple of days she and her sister would be back in Whitewater, Wisconsin. He'd wrap up the Shore investigation, then put in for a transfer to Chicago so he could be near his family and his son. He hadn't been much of a father to Cody the past few years, other than phone calls and summertime visits. He needed to be there for his son, the way his old man had been there for him and his brothers.

Chicago wasn't all that far from Wisconsin, but considering the guilt Bailey harbored about leaving home in the first place, asking her to move even farther away from her sister would be an exercise in futility. He even had his doubts about her staying with her accounting firm in Milwaukee, so the chances of her packing up and moving to Chicago to be with him were slim to none.

So where did that leave them? With just one glorious night between them? Although it was definitely a night he knew he'd never forget, he had no problem admitting that it wasn't enough. Telling himself great sex didn't equate with happily-ever-after was of little use. He couldn't say he loved Bailey, he wasn't even sure what love was any longer. But he did know losing her wasn't an option he even wanted to consider.

Which brought him back to square one.

He let out a long frustrated breath. Thinking about the future was a waste of time. They had to concentrate on the next few hours. He had made sure she was as prepared as he could make her in the small amount of time available. They'd spent a good portion of the day in the gym practicing what she'd already learned, and he'd even shown her a few new techniques, particularly what to do if Shore held a weapon on her. He drove her hard, but she'd remained focused and executed each technique with equal diligence. All they could do now was hope the plan worked and no one made any mistakes. The alternative was unthinkable.

He got to his feet. The peace of the evening did little to ease his mind. Maybe talking to Bailey would do what the quiet of the twilight could not.

He stepped into the house, heading down the corridor to her bedroom. Her door was slightly open, so he pushed it wide and slipped into the room. She sat on the edge of the bed, her back to him, brushing her hair, the long silken strands falling down the back of the pale pink T-shirt that just covered her thighs. Images of wrapping his hands around the blond length flirted on the edges of his consciousness. Heat shot south when he thought of how her hair had been plastered to her back, dripping wet as she'd slipped to her knees in the shower and loved him with her mouth.

Slowly, almost hesitantly, he walked deeper into the room to circle the bed until he stood in front of her. Taking the brush from her hand, he tossed it on the dresser. She looked up at him, her eyes filled with questions and emotion. An emotion he could only name as love.

Her love frightened him. She was decent and kind and trusting, a bright beacon in the dark harbor his life had become since that fateful night three years ago when Jim's and Ashley's lives had ended. He should stay away from her, he should walk away and forget about the emotion shining in her wide blue eyes. He'd bring her nothing but heartache.... Yet, like an addict who'd do just about anything for a fix, he selfishly had to have her one last time.

And God help him, to love her.

He pulled her to her feet and wrapped his arms around her, holding her against him. She snuggled close and laid her hand over his chest, as if trying to physically caress his heart. His heart, where he wanted to believe she belonged to him. Where he could protect her from harm. Where he could keep her close. Where he could love her.

She sighed, the sound sweet and filled with contentment.

Instinct conflicted with tenderness. Instincts he'd relied on for too long told him this would be their last time together. Tenderness, something he hadn't had enough of the past few years, told him they could have a lifetime together.

"I can't make you any promises," he said, running his hands over her back in long sweeping motions.

She pulled back and looked up at him. "I know," she said quietly, her gaze solemn. "But we do have this moment."

Since he'd met her, she'd delivered him one surprise after another, but nothing could have prepared him for her simple acquiescence now. They had no future, but she was right...they did have the moment. And he'd wasted too many moments worrying about their lack of tomorrows.

He gently cupped her face in his hands, carefully rubbing his thumb over her lips. She pulled in a deep breath and closed her eyes. He lowered his head and coaxed her lips open, teasing her with his tongue. When she opened to him, he didn't hesitate, but swept inside to taste her. He groaned when she playfully mated with his tongue in an unspoken promise of passion.

Never taking his lips from hers, he pulled her tighter against him, lifting her until she wrapped her legs around his waist. His hands settled on her bottom to support her, her bare skin hot beneath the long shirt she wore. He needed her, ached with the sweet anticipation that need created. She moaned softly and arched toward him, pressing insistently against him until he thought he'd come out of his skin.

"Are you always this impatient?" he asked with a chuckle against her lips.

"I want you, O'Neill," she said, her voice a husky purr. She nipped playfully at his lips, then soothed the spot with the tip of her tongue. "Now."

He complied, easing them down onto the soft mattress. She slipped her T-shirt over her head and started tugging off his clothes. Exploring his body with her hands and lips, she touched, tasted and drove him dangerously close to madness. He'd wanted to take things slow, to savor every last moment they had together, but she had something completely different in mind. Her insistent touch, her demanding mouth said she wanted it hot and fast.

He gave her what she wanted and stripped out of his clothes, then slid his body with aching slowness over hers before capturing her lips in a deep, tongue tangling kiss. They touched, tasted and loved, neither ashamed of the fierce need that drove them both to the brink.

No stranger to passion, nothing in his life could have prepared him for the deep desire and tender emotions that consumed him when she cradled him between her thighs. She pressed herself against him in unspoken demand, and he complied, sliding deep inside her.

With her arms stretched above her head, she writhed, pulling him deep inside her body until he touched the tip of her womb. With each measured stroke of his body, she pulled him deeper, not just physically, but emotionally. He was lost, and never wanted to return to the world that would eventually tear them apart. He showed her with his body what he couldn't say with words: she was his, and he never wanted to let her go.

He captured her hands, palm to palm, and laced their fingers together. The wild beating of her heart thundered against his chest, matching the pounding behind his own ribs as their bodies met and parted in an ancient rhythm, carrying them to the sweet sensation of a mutual climax.

They dozed, then made love again as the twilight deepened into night. With a final kiss, he reluctantly left her so she could dress for the night ahead.

An hour later, as they drove down the hill to the parking lot where they were scheduled to meet Blake and the others, he knew that no matter what happened in the next few hours, Bailey would always be his.

A SOLID RAP sounded on the back door of the surveillance van, followed by Mason's deep voice. "Bailey, it's me," he called.

"Come in," she said, trying to work the front zipper of the black denim skirt Detective Hammond had asked her to change into when they'd arrived at the meeting place. A small transponder had been sewn into the hem, he'd said, so if she left with Shore, they'd be able to track her.

The back door of the van swung open, and Mason climbed inside, pulling the door closed behind him. "I could use some help," she said over her shoulder. She sucked in a deep breath and held it, managing to inch the zipper up another few notches.

He moved to sit in front of her and pushed her hands out of the way. She pulled in another deep breath and held it, while O'Neill worked the zipper.

She let out the breath she'd been holding and frowned. "What did he do? Shop in the children's department?" she complained, then pulled in another deep breath and managed the button closure. "I can't even squeeze a quarter into the pocket for a phone call."

She adjusted the silky, dragon-red top Detective Hammond had given her to wear. Thin spaghetti straps held the top in place, but the low-scooped neckline barely covered her breasts. She felt exposed and vulnerable when she needed every ounce of confidence she possessed.

"Everyone's in place," he told her, fiddling with the instrument panel of the surveillance equipment. "We've got two officers in the bar. Find John

and sit next to him. He'll be wearing a red flannel
shirt and a Dodgers' ball cap. Don't talk to him, just
order something and wait for Shore or one of his
people to make contact."

"I know," she said, mildly irritated, bending to
try to loosen the tight denim. "We've been over this
already."

"You're not to initiate anything this time. Let
Shore do the talking so we can get everything on
tape." His voice was filled with authority, but she
understood. They shared the same fears and concern.

She swallowed her irritation and sat beside him
on the cushioned bench. "I know," she said, slipping her arm through his. "I promise to follow directions this time."

He looked at her, a deep frown marring his forehead. "And you're not to leave with anyone except
Shore. He might send the Butcher or even Roxanne
for you. You're to wait for him."

She nodded because she couldn't speak. Even in
the dim light from the instrument panel, she saw
the affection and concern in his amber eyes. It gave
her hope that she hadn't been imagining things and
that maybe, just maybe, he really did return her
feelings.

He turned his attention back to the instrument
panel, picked up a headset and slipped it on before
making a few adjustments to the panel. "If he
shows and you go with him, don't do or say anything stupid. No mention of street names. It's a
dead giveaway that someone is listening. If you
leave, we'll be right behind you, and we've got the
tracking device." He pointed to the computer

screen and a small flashing light appeared. He struck a few keys and their location appeared on the screen.

"Now say something so we can test the wire."

"What about my sister? How do I find out where she is?"

"If he's got Leslie, we're pretty certain Shore will take you to the same place he's holding her." He slid a few buttons in opposite directions and kept his attention on the panel. "No one has seen or heard of a new girl on the streets, so there's a good chance he's holding her."

"What if she's already been...you know." The thought of what Leslie might have suffered the past few weeks left her cold. She couldn't bear to think of her sister being sold as if she was a commodity.

O'Neill slipped off the headset and put it aside. He turned to face her, gently lifting her chin with his forefinger until she looked at him. Determination, and some other deep emotion crossed his features. "We'll find her, Bailey," he said softly. "I promise you, we'll find her."

"Mason?"

"Yeah?"

"No matter what happens tonight, I want you to know that I love you. Can you promise me you won't forget that?"

When he kissed her, she had her answer.

BY THE TIME Bailey walked the block and a half to Shadee's, her feet were protesting from the red stilettos she'd worn. She wished she'd brought the lower-heeled boots. Not only were they more comfortable, but if for some reason she had to run or move quickly, the high heels would definitely impede her. She really didn't care what sort of fashion statement she made, comfort and mobility took precedence. She just wished she'd thought of it sooner.

She slipped inside the smoke-filled bar and waited for her eyes to adjust to the dim light. The acrid stench of stale tobacco and bitter alcohol assailed her senses and burned her eyes. She peered into the room, but saw no sign of Roxanne or Shore. She spotted John Reynolds sitting in the corner of the bar with his back to the wall and one leg propped over the empty bar stool next to him. A half-empty amber bottle was clutched loosely in his hand, but she was pretty sure the yellowed potted palm next to him had done all the drinking. The Dodgers' ball cap rode low over his forehead, shielding his eyes. If she didn't know better, she'd have assumed he was sleeping, but her recent exposure to the undercover officers told her John was alert and ready for action should the need arise.

Carefully, she picked her way through the crowd to the bar. A bold customer patted her on the behind. It took every ounce of willpower to ignore him rather than give him the scathing dressing-down he deserved. Instead, she approached John and, she thought, safety.

"Excuse me," she said to him. "Is this seat taken?"

John grunted in reply and dropped his foot to the floor. He lifted the bottle in salute, then turned and braced his arms on the stained bar.

Climbing onto the stool was no easy task thanks

to Detective Hammond's fashion selection. She maneuvered onto the seat, tugging at the hem of the black denim. Beneath her fingertips, she felt the small transmitter, about half the size of a dime and nearly as thin. She tried to find comfort in knowing that O'Neill was listening, but her bravado of the past few days began to wane. Not only was her own life at risk should they be discovered, but possibly that of her sister's, as well. If she managed to get inside Shore's hiding place, she couldn't let him learn that she and Leslie were sisters. If he did, there was every chance they'd meet the same fateful end as poor William Greene.

The grisly bartender from the previous evening was on duty. When he sauntered over, she ordered a 7UP with a shot of Cuervo on the side. He shrugged, then delivered her request, slapping the drinks down in front of her on a napkin printed with ribald jokes before snagging the ten-dollar bill she offered him.

She sipped the soda, ignoring the tequila, and looked around the room. Those patronizing the blues club tonight were more boisterous than the people from the previous evening. When the four-piece combo took the stage, the noise level of the crowd increased in an effort to be heard over the sultry rhythms of the band.

With nothing to do but wait, her mind naturally wandered to O'Neill. She thought of their earlier lovemaking, and how tender he'd been. No matter what he'd said or hadn't said, he loved her.

They hadn't used protection, but she didn't think there was much of a chance of her becoming pregnant. No matter what they'd told her in high school, she wasn't quite that naive. And as she'd told O'Neill in the early morning hours when they'd first made love, they were at the safest point in her cycle, and there was little risk of pregnancy. Not that she'd mind having a child with O'Neill, but it certainly would complicate their already complicated relationship.

They hadn't spoken of what would happen once Devlin Shore was behind bars where he belonged. But O'Neill constantly reminded her that they had no future together.

She didn't believe that for a moment. They had more than a future together, they had a lifetime together, and whether he realized it or not, that was exactly what she had planned. A lifetime with O'Neill.

She finished her soda, then signaled Grisly for another. She felt sorry for Mason and Blake, sitting inside the hot surveillance van. As much as she hated being in the blues club, at least the air-conditioning helped cool the place.

She searched the crowd again, but found nothing out of the ordinary. Her gaze slipped to the corridor that Roxanne had disappeared down the night before, wondering what, or more important, who, she might find if she ventured in that direction.

"SHE'S MOVIN'." Kate Morgan's voice came over the two-way surveillance system.

"Son of a bitch," Mason said. "I told her to stay put. Where's she headed?"

"Looks like the little girls' room, O'Neill. Don't sweat it, I'm right behind her."

Mason glanced at his partner resting casually on

the padded bench against the interior wall of the van. Blake's legs were stretched in front of him and his hands were laced over his stomach. A grin tugged at his lips. "She's a stubborn one, isn't she?"

"I ought to break her neck for this," Mason grumbled. "Talk to me, Kate."

"She's in the corridor," Kate said, her voice a hushed whisper. "Uh-oh. We've got company."

Mason snagged the binoculars from the bench and zeroed in on Shadee's. Nothing unusual. He scanned the street, looking for a sign that Shore had arrived. Nothing.

He heard Bailey's sharp intake of breath followed by the voice that had haunted his dreams for far too long.

Devlin Shore.

13

"LOOKING FOR SOMEONE?"

Bailey stared at the man who'd never been far from her thoughts the past few weeks. Until now, the closest she'd been to him was a photograph, or from a distance, the night he'd flashed a lethal-looking knife in front of Roxanne's face. Up close and personal, Devlin Shore was a very attractive man. He was tall, almost as tall as O'Neill, with wide shoulders evident beneath a dark blue silk suit. Raven-black hair, smoothed back from his face and gathered into a ponytail, emphasized high cheekbones and a straight patrician nose. He looked like any other well-dressed businessman, someone she might run into at her own office. He looked polished and refined. Except for his eyes. His eyes were cold, almost black in color, like that of a great white shark with malice on his mind.

She thought of O'Neill listening to every word spoken. Her heart pounded beneath her ribs and she wondered if he could hear that, as well. Telling herself that O'Neill and the others were there to protect her didn't alleviate the fear stealing over her. The knowledge didn't stop her hands from shaking, either.

Gathering her courage, she raked Shore with her gaze, then gave him her best sultry smile.

"Maybe," she replied saucily, despite the nerves churning in her stomach, "but not just anyone."

Kate Morgan brushed past her and slipped into the ladies' room. Bailey couldn't help wondering if Kate was listening on the other side of the door, and took comfort knowing that the female officer was close at hand.

Shore's cold eyes slid over her, traveling slowly from her toes and up, until he finally looked her in the eye. Suppressing a shudder proved difficult, and she resisted the urge to cover her body with her hands.

"Who are you?" he asked, his voice as smooth as his suit.

She hefted her bag higher onto her shoulder and fiddled with the strap, then rudely snapped her gum. "They call me Sugar."

He lifted his hand and ran his finger over her other shoulder and down her arm, his touch light, but she sensed the threat. Regardless of the hours she'd spent learning various self-defense techniques, no amount of training could keep the gooseflesh from her arms.

"Is that because you're as sweet as your name?"

She shrugged, but she really wanted to take a step back. That was a luxury she couldn't afford. She was sure this man had her sister, or at least knew where she could find Leslie. "Could be," she said, hoping the grin wasn't the grimace she suspected.

He straightened and eyed her again, critically this time as if she was nothing but an object available for purchase. "Well, Sugar, my associate tells me you're looking for protection."

She shrugged again. She hadn't seen Roxanne since she'd arrived at Shadee's, and wondered how Shore knew she was the one. "Yeah, well, it's gettin' tough out there tryin' to make a livin', ya know. Be nice to have somebody screenin' the clients. Roxanne says you're a pimp. That true?"

"*Pimp* is an ugly word, don't you think? We're in the sales business, Sugar."

A door opened and Shore quieted, glancing over his shoulder as Kate Morgan strolled back into the corridor. Bailey glanced in her direction, but the undercover officer sashayed past, giving Shore a seductive look.

"I have something that people want," he said, his gaze narrowing when Kate moved on to the crowded bar. "That makes me more of an agent or perhaps a business manager. Do you need a manager, Sugar?"

Bailey frowned at him, hoping she looked irritated. "Isn't that what I just said, Slick?" She crossed her arms over her chest and snapped her gum. "Yeah, I could use a *manager*. I'm tired of gettin' ripped off."

"Why don't we go to my office where we can discuss this privately?" Shore gently placed his hand on her elbow and steered her away from the wall.

She shrugged out of his grasp. "I don't go nowhere with nobody I don't know."

He smiled, but she detected no warmth. "The name's Shore. Devlin Shore."

She snapped her gum a couple of times. "Okay, Devlin Shore, agent extraordinaire. But we're only talkin' business. Don't think you're gettin' nuttin' for free."

He chuckled, then took her elbow once again to steer her toward the back of the blues club. "My dear Sugar, I wouldn't dream of it. You're perfectly safe with me. After all, this is an arrangement of safety, is it not?"

"Might be," she said, looking behind her. From the corridor, she spotted John Reynolds where she'd left him at the bar. The ball cap was still pulled low over his eyes, but she knew he was watching her like a hawk. The thought gave her a modicum of comfort.

Shore led her to a thick walnut-stained door. He rapped twice on the door and it swung open.

Bailey swallowed a sharp gasp. *The Butcher*. O'Neill had told her she'd know him the minute she saw him, and he hadn't been lying. Here stood the obvious muscle behind the brains in the operation. Bald, close to six and a half feet tall, and nearly as wide, his appearance alone was pure intimidation.

For all of two seconds, she wished she'd listened to O'Neill and had let the professionals handle this. But the notion fled when she thought of her sister. Instead of cowering and running to the safety of O'Neill's arms the way she really wanted to, she swallowed her fear and stepped past Shore into the dingy office.

Poor overhead fluorescent lighting cast the room in a hazy glow, doing nothing to tame the garish red-and-gold shag carpeting or worn imitation-leather furnishings. Shore led her to a red chair and urged her to sit before nodding to the Butcher to close the door.

She set her bag on the chair beside her and

looked around the office. "Don't look like you're doin' such good business if ya' gotta use this dump for an office."

Her gaze rested momentarily on the Butcher and his chilling ice blue eyes watching her intently. He stood with his arms crossed and his back to the door. To keep others out, or her inside, she couldn't be sure. Had this monstrosity of a man been the one to convince her sister to come with him? From the looks of him, she didn't think Leslie would have gone anywhere with this guy. Had they taken Leslie against her will? Anything was possible, she realized, even kidnapping.

Shore leaned against a cheap walnut desk, crossing his feet at the ankles. By all appearances, he looked relaxed, but Bailey had the impression he was constantly on alert. "I'm only borrowing it for the moment. It's much too noisy for conversation inside the bar. You never know who could be listening. Would you like a drink?"

Fear clogged her throat. Anyone could be listening, and they were, a few hundred yards away in the back of a stuffy surveillance van. She leaned back in the chair and tried to cross her legs, but the tight skirt wouldn't allow it. "I ain't here for a tea party. Let's talk business."

"Sugar, I can offer you protection. In fact, from what I've seen, I'm confident you'd be an asset."

"Whaddya mean?" she asked, but she had a feeling deep in her gut that she knew where this conversation was headed. O'Neill had said to keep him talking, and that's just what she intended to do, hoping to get something on tape that O'Neill could use to put Shore away for good.

She stood, her heels sinking into the shag carpeting. She hefted her bag over her shoulder and struggled to maintain her balance. "I don't do kinky stuff, so you can just forget it."

The coldness in Shore's eyes deepened and she suppressed a shiver. "Sit down, Sugar," he ordered, the silkiness of his voice slipping to reveal a hardness she suspected was never far from the surface. "What I plan to offer you will be the chance of a lifetime. How would you like to have just about anything your heart desires?"

Was this the line he'd fed her sister? Had Leslie fallen prey to the silky smoothness of Shore, or had she been forced to comply against her will?

"Who wouldn't?" she answered, perching on the edge of the seat. "But I live in the real world. Life don't work that way for girls like me."

"Oh, but it can, Sugar. And it will. Trust me," he said, his eyes and voice menacing.

She glared at him. "I don't trust nobody."

She glanced from Shore to the Incredible Bulk blocking the door. If she jumped on his offer, would he become suspicious? Shore wasn't a stupid man. She had to put up some resistance, didn't she?

"My mama always said if somethin's too good to be true, then it is. I think I'll pass." She stood again and moved toward the door. The Butcher shifted, and for the flash of an instant she thought he'd let her go, until he reached inside his leather jacket and leveled his gun at her.

Bailey swallowed hard, and backed up a step. Her legs brushed against the chair and she sat. She had known she'd be facing danger, and she hadn't really been naive enough to believe guns wouldn't be involved.

"I see we understand each other," Shore said in that silky voice that was beginning to grate on her nerves.

"Yeah, you're gonna shoot me if I don't go with you."

Shore hauled her to her feet. "Of course not," he said, taking her bag from her and tossing it to his *compadre.* "You'll come of your own free will. However, there is another option."

He let the threat sink in, giving her no choice but to go quietly. Telling herself this is what they wanted, what she and O'Neill had prepared for, did nothing to calm the wild beating of her heart or the stark fear creeping through her veins turning them to ice.

"I want you to come with me, and I always get what I want," Shore said, then nodded to the Butcher, who opened the door. "You're a valuable commodity, Sugar," he said, guiding her into the hallway. "Do you know what a commodity is?"

"Yeah, sure," she said, looking down the hallway to the bar. The seat John had occupied was empty, and her stomach bottomed out.

They stopped at the rear exit. Bailey craned her neck to look back toward the bar again. There was no sign of John or Kate. She warred with the panic trying to take hold. *Remain calm*, she told herself firmly. *You're getting what you wanted, and this sleazeball is going to take you to Leslie.*

She hoped.

Shore's grip on her arm tightened and she winced. "Then we understand each other?"

She looked from him to the muscle with the weapon and nodded.

"Shall we?" Shore asked, opening the door. A long, black limousine waited. The Butcher stepped forward and nudged her inside.

"Well, when you put it that way," she said, and slipped out the back door of Shadee's.

"THEY'RE MOVING," Blake said, punching computer keys. "He's taking her."

Mason kept the binoculars trained on the front door of Shadee's. He'd been tense all night, his instincts telling him the sting was going down as planned. He hated Bailey being near Shore, and had heard the fear in her voice, barely covered by her false bravado. Fury had poured through him when he heard Shore's thinly veiled threats, and it took every ounce of training for him not to charge into the bar and put an end to the operation.

"Where the hell is everyone?" Mason barked.

"I don't know," Blake grumbled. "Kate, anything?"

"They slipped out the back door into a limo." Kate's voice crackled over the transmitter. "I'm with John in the car. We're waiting for them to pull out."

A few moments later, a long black limousine turned onto Hollywood Boulevard and sped past them. Mason wanted nothing more than to jump into the driver's seat of the van and tail them personally, but there were other officers set to follow them. The thought did little to ease his mind, nor did the steady bleep of the tracking giving them Bailey's approximate location.

Someone knocked on the rear door of the van. "It's Crandall," he called, and Blake opened the door.

"You saw them?" he asked Mason, climbing into the van.

"Yeah," he said, but he hadn't heard a sound from Bailey in the last five minutes. He didn't like it. "Get behind the wheel. We can't let her get too far out of range or we'll lose her."

"This is Kate. Target just entered the on-ramp for the 101 northbound."

"Keep with them," Mason ordered the other officer. "We're on our way."

And then he heard her, along with the slight quaver in her voice, and knew she was scared. Her fear crept through him, and he fought to remain focused on the job at hand. His goal was to bring down Shore and hopefully find her sister. But the bastard had Bailey, and if anything happened to her, Mason silently vowed that Shore wouldn't live to see another sunrise.

"I'VE NEVER BEEN in a limo before," Bailey said, using the excuse to look around. The doors were locked and the windows more than likely bulletproof. She flipped open a hatch and found a cellular phone.

"You got a bar in here?" she asked, snapping the hatch and opening another cabinet to find a laptop computer. What could someone like Shore possibly need with a laptop? she wondered. No disk sat in the drive, but she was sure if she had the time to look around, she could find one. Whether or not it would tell them anything, she didn't know, but it was worth keeping in mind.

"My dear, you do amuse me. So much more than your sister. You know, I think you'll bring me a very good price."

Her stomach sank and she fought to breathe normally. *He knew.* God help them, he knew. How, she had no idea, but the jig was up, unless she could convince him otherwise. "Sister?"

"Yes, Miss Grayson, your sister." The smoothness evaporated, leaving only cold hatred on his face. "You're no twenty-dollar hooker. The family resemblance to your little sibling is quite uncanny."

She snapped her gum and cocked her head to the side to study him. The coldness in his eyes made her shiver. "Sorry, Slick, but I ain't followin' ya."

Shore looked to his partner in crime, who pressed a button on the panel, lowering the dark window separating the driver from the passengers. "I think we'll sell them as a pair," Shore said, a grin transforming his expression from one of cold hatred to mocking evil. "A tidy little sum, don't you agree?" Shore called over his shoulder to the driver.

"Absolutely," the driver said, looking into the rearview mirror.

Bailey stared at the driver's reflection in disbelief. Slowly, the pieces fell into place.

Someone on the inside had tipped off Shore.

Mason's words sprang to the forefront of her mind, along with the details he'd given her of the previous sting. Shore knew who she was and had been expecting them, and the only way he could have known was if someone had provided him with the information. Mason's instincts had once again been right on; Shore had been tipped off again.

By one of L.A.'s finest.

"Oh my God," Bailey whispered, seconds before a flash of pain to the back of her head hurled her into a dark, black abyss.

A LOUD CRACK filtered through the headset, followed by dead silence. Fear clawed at Mason's gut. His worst nightmare had resurfaced. They'd been found out.

"Dammit, they found the wire," he barked, ripping off the headset and throwing it across the van.

Blake swore vividly, then punched a series of buttons on the keyboard. "They haven't found the tracking unit. Look, she's still moving."

Mason stared at the green image bleeping on the screen as it moved along the busy Los Angeles freeway. He rubbed his hand down his face. If anything happened to Bailey... He couldn't afford to think about Bailey being harmed. He had to remain focused or he could lose her forever. And losing Bailey was something he refused to even consider.

But nothing could prevent the images of Ashley Adams's body from flooding his mind. Only this time, he didn't see Ashley's youthful face. Instead, he saw Bailey, and his blood ran cold. "We have to get her out of there," he told Blake.

His partner laid a hand on his shoulder in a gesture of comfort. Mason didn't want comfort. He wanted Bailey safe. He wanted her beside him for the rest of their lives. He wanted to build a life with her, grow old with her. Dammit, he wanted to let her know what she'd suspected all along, that he loved her. Unless he got to her soon, he might never have the chance to tell her what was in his heart.

"We'll find her, partner," Blake said quietly. "I promise you. We'll find her. Kate's tailing her and she's one of the best. She won't lose her."

The thought did little to calm his racing heart, or the cold fury surrounding him. But if anyone knew Devlin Shore or could second-guess his actions, it would be Kate Morgan, since she'd been in on the investigation from the beginning.

Blake slipped his headset on and adjusted the mouthpiece. "Kate, come back," he said quietly.

Blake looked at Mason, his expression serious. "Kate?" he said again. Blake made a few adjustments to the instrument panel. "Kate, do you read?"

Mason turned to the monitor, watching as the green cursor inched toward the downtown cloverleaf, then exited the freeway. He gave the coordinates to Crandall.

"Kate? Do you read?"

An odd note in Blake's voice caught Mason's attention, and he tensed. Something wasn't right, off-kilter, and all to familiar. History was repeating itself. The night Jim and Ashley had been murdered, an officer had lost radio contact for a brief period of time.

He thought about the investigation, the officers involved. Until Jim's death, only one other officer had been involved in the Shore investigation.

Kate Morgan.

She had been involved right from the beginning. Jim had trusted her, had worked with her on other cases, and his partner's word had been enough for Mason. But as he thought about it now, he should have realized that something was amiss when he learned that Kate had gone to Lieutenant Forbes and specifically requested the assignment to the Shore case.

Blake slipped off the headset and calmly set it on the bench beside him. "She's not answering," he said.

"She won't," Mason answered, disgust rippling through him in waves. Now he understood how Shore had always managed to be one step ahead of them. "She's in bed with Shore."

"Figuratively or literally?"

"Does it matter?" Mason asked, not really expecting a reply.

Blake turned his attention to the monitor, but not before Mason caught the fury brewing in his partner's eyes. No one liked a dirty cop.

"They're stopping," Blake said, then issued a new set of coordinates to Crandall while Mason placed a call to Lieutenant Forbes, advising him of Kate's suspected involvement with Shore.

Five minutes later, Crandall slowed the vehicle. "It's an empty lot," he called to the back of the van. "You sure they're here?"

"This is it," Blake answered, tapping the screen.

Mason carefully stepped toward the front of the van. "Turn in here," he said, indicating a convenience store on the corner beside the lot. He waited until Crandall stopped the van, then palmed his weapon. "Keep it running."

He slipped out of the van and surveyed the area. Behind the lot stood an abandoned warehouse, the windows busted out long ago by kids practicing their rock-pitching skills or maybe transients looking for a place away from the Santa Ana winds common during the winter months. In the distance he could hear the constant hum of vehicles that sped along the freeway overpass.

"I'll check out the warehouse," Mason said. "You scan the lot," he ordered Blake.

He bent low and ran along the edge of the lot, until he reached the fence surrounding the warehouse. Slipping through a gap in the chain-link fence, he stayed low and crept up to the concrete building. The area was deserted, but he checked the perimeter for any sign of life, just to be safe.

Nothing.

After checking the doors and windows of the building and coming up empty-handed, he started back toward the fence. The blare of a horn caught his attention. He crouched, and looked toward the van. Blake stood near the rear door, signaling for him to hurry.

Mason broke into a run. Blake had found something.

"Over here," Blake said as he neared the van. "Fresh tracks."

Mason kept silent, afraid if he spoke, he'd reveal his worst fear—that Bailey had been taken from him.

Please, God. No, he prayed.

He almost missed it, and if it hadn't been for the

bright red pump tangled in a tumbleweed, they might've searched the area for hours before finding anything.

Mason crouched and plucked the items from the tumbleweed, ignoring the burrs that dug into his skin. Rage boiled inside him, but he corralled his emotions and buried them, knowing he couldn't allow himself to feel anything.

He stood, a deadly calm settling over him as he carried back to the van what was left of the black denim skirt and red silk blouse Bailey had been wearing.

14

CONSCIOUSNESS RETURNED, and with it, a pounding headache. Bailey opened her eyes as the black fog surrounding her parted. Incandescent light bathed the room in a soft glow. Without moving, she glanced around the room. She was in a bedroom, an elegantly furnished room, she thought, noting the pale peach canopy overhead and the soft down-filled comforter covering her. She could see a window, and outside the sky was dark.

A movement caught her attention and she slowly turned her head on the pillow. Sitting on an overstuffed chair, her legs tucked beneath her, was Leslie. She kept her gaze on the door and chewed at her thumbnail, a habit telling of her anxiety.

Relief washed over Bailey. Her sister was alive, and nothing else mattered for the moment. Not Shore and his evil plans, not discovering Kate Morgan was in with Shore, or even the fact that she and Les could both end up dead before the sun rose.

"Les?" she whispered.

Leslie straightened and neared the bed, her expression somber. Maturity and concern had replaced the perky and somewhat selfish child she'd known all her life. She'd changed, and it broke Bailey's heart.

Leslie sat tentatively on the edge of the bed. "I'm sorry, Bailey," she said, keeping her voice low.

Holding the sheet to her chest, Bailey pushed herself up and clasped her sister's hand. "All that matters is you're alive, and we're together. I'm going to get us out of here, so don't worry…. What is this place? Where are we?"

Leslie shook her head, her long blond hair falling over her shoulder. "I don't know. Bailey, I really screwed up this time," she said. Tears choked her voice, but she fought valiantly to prevent them from falling.

Bailey wrapped one arm around her sister. "Shh, we'll talk about that later. Let's concentrate on getting out of here."

Leslie stiffened and pulled away. "There's no way out," she said. "I've tried. We're watched constantly."

Leslie's calm, serious demeanor concerned Bailey. She wanted her sister happy again, but right now she needed to find a way to get them as far from Devlin Shore as possible. "Who is 'we'?"

"There are four other girls here," Leslie said.

"Have they hurt you?"

"No. They've been 'saving' us for an auction."

"Auction?" she asked hesitantly.

Leslie nodded. "Remember the cattle auctions Dad used to take us to when we were kids? It's like that. Roxanne said they're going to have an auction and they're gonna sell me. She said they're gonna sell you, too, along with the others."

Bailey stared at her sister in disbelief. What Mason and his partner had believed was in fact reality. Shore *was* selling girls on the black market, only it was much worse than any of them had imagined. "When?" she asked, appalled.

Leslie stood and circled the bed. "I don't know for sure," she said, "but I heard them say something about tomorrow night."

"Do you know where?"

"No, but I think we're leaving here. Roxanne told us our 'new lives' would start tomorrow."

Bailey shuddered at the thought of what could happen if she didn't at least get to a phone and try to reach Mason. What she'd tell him, she had no idea. She didn't have a clue as to their whereabouts.

Bailey climbed out of the bed and wrapped the comforter around her. She had no idea where her clothes were, but she couldn't exactly say she missed wearing the uncomfortable skirt Detective Hammond had given her.

"I need something to wear," she told her sister, then crossed the room to the door, her toes sinking into the thick peach carpeting. The door was locked, as she'd suspected.

Leslie took a sweat suit from the top of the bureau and tossed it on the bed. "Roxanne left these."

She dropped the comforter and pulled the hooded sweatshirt over her head, then looked at the blank television screen in the corner. By the time she stepped into the sweatpants, an idea had taken shape.

She flipped off the lamp and walked through the darkened room to the window. Looking out into the predawn sky, she knew she had no other choice. As she suspected, they were on the second floor of what seemed to be a Beverly Hills mansion.

Peering into the night, she saw a swimming pool illuminated by the slowly waning moon. Beyond looked to be a tennis court.

"Bailey? How's Mom?"

Bailey turned to face her sister, her heart twisting at the pain etched around Leslie's blue eyes, evident even in the moonlight-shadowed room. "She's worried about you. We've all been worried. Especially Ned."

Leslie looked down at the floor. "I was so stupid. I don't know why I did it."

Bailey closed the short distance between them and laid her hands over Leslie's shoulders. "Why did you run away?"

Leslie lifted her gaze, her eyes filled with tears. "I was mad at Mom for marrying Ned. It was so soon after Dad died, I guess I just figured she couldn't have loved Dad, or even us. And Ned was always trying to act like he was my dad, you know. Like I said, I was stupid."

"How did you end up here?"

"I got off the bus downtown, and well, I was scared and I guess it showed. I was trying to figure out what to do next and this really nice lady, Roxanne, came up to me at the bus station and we started talking. She offered me a place to stay and a job. I had no idea just what kind of job she meant."

Bailey wrapped her arms around her sister and held her close. "We're going to get out of here, Les," she whispered, smoothing her sister's hair. "You'll be able to put it all behind you, I promise."

Leslie pulled away, giving Bailey the distinct impression her youthful sister had been taken away from her forever. In her place was a young woman filled with regrets for her actions.

"You can't make me that kind of promise. It's not yours to make. Look, I screwed up. I can handle it. I just want to go home."

With nothing left to say, Bailey crossed to the window again and tried the latch. "It's open," she whispered.

Leslie shook her head. "No way, Bailey. We're on the second floor."

"I just need to make it to a room with a phone. I'll be careful," she said, slowly sliding the window open. Next, she carefully removed the protective screen and propped it against the wall. "Did you see anything of this place when Roxanne brought you here?"

"A little. Mostly we stay in our rooms. Roxanne or some guy brings us food and stuff. These aren't nice people, Bailey. If they find you, they'll kill you."

Bailey tried not to think of what could happen, only of the task ahead. "Turn on the television," she instructed Leslie. "Try to find a talk show or something so they think we're talking."

Bailey checked her watch while Leslie turned on the set. "We've got about an hour until sunrise. If I can get to a phone and back, we'll be okay. Now tell me what you know about the layout of this place."

MASON SAT on the sofa in Lieutenant Forbes's office. With his elbows braced on his knees, he clasped his hands around a foam cup filled with cold coffee. He felt numb, as if a part of him had died.

Bailey was missing, gone without a trace. Kate Morgan had disappeared with Shore, and no one had seen or heard from Reynolds since he'd told them he was going to meet Kate and wait to follow Shore. They'd sent out a pair of squad cars to canvas the area surrounding Shadee's to search for Reynolds, but Mason already had a bad feeling about the vice cop's chances of survival.

History had repeated itself. His world was crashing down around him, and all he could do was stare into a cup filled with cold coffee.

Mason looked up when Lieutenant Forbes entered the office and saw the fierce scowl on the man's face. "They found Reynolds," he said, tossing a file on the desk in front of Blake. "Two bullets in the chest. He's alive, barely, and on his way to Cedars."

Mason nodded. At least Reynolds was alive, for the time being.

"We've got an APB out on Shore, the Butcher and Officer Morgan. We'll find Ms. Grayson, O'Neill," Forbes said in an uncharacteristic show of compassion.

Mason set the cup on the floor between his feet and ran his hands down his face. He was a cop. The entire Los Angeles Police Department was at his disposal, yet he felt completely helpless. They'd sent out every available patrol officer, called in more detectives and were rousing every snitch they had, and still they'd turned up nothing on Shore or his location. He was tired and his eyes felt grainy. He needed sleep, but realized it would be impossible until he knew Bailey was safe. The minute they had a lead, anything, he'd be on it, and he didn't think even God could help Devlin Shore when he got his hands on the bastard.

The phone rang and Forbes reached for it. "Hold on," he said, and held out the receiver to Mason. "O'Neill. It's your girl."

Mason bolted from the sofa and snagged the phone from Forbes. "Where are you?" he barked into the phone.

"Mason," she said, her tone low and hushed.

Mason closed his eyes, relief sweeping over him at the sound of her voice. She was alive. "Where are you, sweetheart?" he asked around the sudden lump in his throat.

"I don't know. Somewhere in Beverly Hills, I think. Mason, you and Blake were right. Shore's selling girls into white slavery. There's an auction tomorrow night, but I don't know where. I found something, too. It might help you."

Instinct took over where emotion threatened to strangle him. "Get me a trace!" he ordered Blake. "Now, dammit!"

Blake pushed out of the chair and bolted from the room, his usual soft-spoken manner forgotten as he began issuing orders to set up the trace.

"I've got to hurry."

His gut twisted at the fear in her voice. When this was over, he swore he'd do everything in his power to make her happy, and he damn sure wouldn't be letting her out of his sight any time soon. "Sweetheart, listen to me. Set the phone down, but don't hang up. We're setting up a trace."

"Okay," she whispered. "Mason, I found Leslie. She's okay. They haven't hurt her."

He listened while she briefly told him how her sister came to be in Shore's clutches. The story was all too familiar. Young kids hitting L.A. hoping for a fresh start and not having a clue how to take care of themselves.

"I'm going to find you," he said when she finished with the sketchy details.

"I love you, Mason," she whispered.

"I love you, too, sweetheart," he said, but the line had gone dead.

"SHE'S OUT THERE and no one knows where." The five minutes that had passed since they'd been cut off felt like five hours. Five minutes that could have disastrous results.

"O'Neill, take it easy." Blake returned to the office, a printout in his hands. "We have the general vicinity. They're holed up in Beverly Hills."

"That's not good enough," he roared. "Even Bailey knew they were in Beverly Hills. We need an address."

He spun on his heel and headed toward the door. If he had to search every mansion in Beverly Hills to get her back, then that's just what he was going to do. But he couldn't sit and wait. The waiting, and worrying, was killing him.

"Where are you going?" Forbes asked.

"To find Bailey," he answered, reaching for the doorknob.

"Where are you going to look?" the lieutenant asked. "The line was cut before we could get the location."

The phone on the desk jangled. "What?" Forbes shouted into the receiver. He listened, then quietly thanked the caller before hanging up. "Shore's pilot just filed a flight plan."

Blake tossed the map he'd been reviewing on the desk. "To where?"

"Florida."

Blake shoved his hands into the pockets of his neatly pressed trousers. "He's leaving the country. My bet is the Caribbean."

Mason pulled open the door. "Let's go," he said to Blake, and headed across the squad room. Finally, a lead that would take him to Bailey.

"O'Neill," Forbes called after him. "Stay out of it. You're too involved."

Mason turned and glared at his superior. "Damn straight I'm involved. That son of a bitch has Bailey."

Forbes crossed his arms over his chest and braced his feet apart. "Let Hammond and the others handle it," he said in a firm tone. "That's an order, O'Neill."

There was no way he was going to let someone else "handle it." There was more at stake here than bringing down Devlin Shore. There was more involved than an old score to settle with a cop-killing bastard. This time, Shore had gone too far. This time, Shore had something that belonged to him—Bailey.

Mason reached inside his shirt and tugged on the silver chain he wore to keep his badge under his clothes. He lifted the chain, slipped it over his head and tossed it on a nearby desk.

"What do you think you're doing?" Forbes asked.

Mason ignored him. He flipped the snap holding his shoulder holster in place, and pulled it from his arm, then carefully set his service pistol on the desk beside his shield. He crossed the short distance separating them, ignoring the shocked expression on Blake's face.

"Shove your order, Lieutenant."

"What the hell do you think you're doing?" Forbes asked, his low voice filled with anger and disbelief. "I could have your badge for this, O'Neill."

"You already do. I quit," Mason said, then spun on his heel and left the squad room.

"I DO HOPE you enjoy warmer climes, Miss Grayson. How does life in the Arabian desert sound to you?"

As the limousine pulled up behind another waiting beside the jet, Bailey glanced over at the tarmac. Beside her, Leslie didn't say a word, but her pale face spoke volumes. They were far from the terminal, in what she assumed was a private section of the Burbank Airport. In the bright morning sunshine, she saw Kate Morgan ushering the other girls from the limo at gunpoint. They huddled together, clinging to one another for support.

If she didn't think of something quickly, they'd soon be on their way to a Middle Eastern country where women's rights were second only to that of the sacred camel or scorpion. "You'll never get away with this, you know," she said, turning her attention back to Shore.

He chuckled, a sound with more malice than mirth, filling the interior of the luxurious car. "Oh, but I will," he said arrogantly. "I have for some time now. Your friends in blue are nostalgically reminiscent of the Keystone Kops. I mean, really, sending in a sweet child like yourself to deal with me. It's quite humorous when you think about it, don't you agree?"

Bailey stuffed her hands into the front pocket of the sweatshirt. Not because her hands were cold, or even trembling, but to reassure herself she still had the disk she'd found in the office of Shore's mansion, where she'd used the phone. She hadn't had time to run the disk to see what type of information it contained, but the label indicated a computerized accounting program she was familiar with and had used in the past. The chances of Shore keeping his nefarious transactions on a disk were high, because in her experience, everyone, low-life criminals included, liked to watch their money grow. She was banking on Shore being no different.

She clutched the disk in her hand, and prayed. "No, actually I don't agree."

Shore reached into his jacket and pulled out a gun, aiming it at her chest. "Make sure the girls are loaded onto the plane, Butch. Miss Grayson and I have some business to discuss. And take her sister."

Leslie looked at her anxiously, but Bailey nodded. She still hadn't come up with a plan, and time was running out. Once they were alone, Shore inclined his head toward the opened car door. "Out, Miss Grayson. We're going for a little walk."

This is it, she thought. Time was up.

WITHOUT THE BENEFIT of sirens and the entire L.A.P.D. behind him, Mason had to use his wits to find a way onto the tarmac. If anyone was keeping score, grand theft auto and trespassing were among the lesser charges he'd be facing when all was said and done.

He easily spotted the private jet and two limousines at the far end of the airport, but had no way of approaching without being spotted. He needed a cover, and fast.

Cover, and luck, presented itself in the guise of a United Airlines ball cap sitting on the seat of a motorized luggage cart. He slipped the cap on his head, then hijacked the full luggage cart before speeding across the tarmac to the waiting plane.

The cold fury that had embraced him for the past few hours kept a tight hold on him as he neared the jet in time to see the Butcher pushing a girl with long blond hair up steps and into the plane. He scanned the area, wondering how he was going to board the plane, when he spotted Bailey with Shore.

Rage crashed over him in hot waves. He steered the cart in their direction with one hand, pulling his spare gun from the holster wedged against his back. He leveled the gun on Shore, then killed the luggage cart's engine.

"Hold it right there, Shore, and I just might let you live."

Shore spun, snaking his arm around Bailey to hold her in front of him. He used her as a shield, his gun pressing against her temple. Mason knew if he could get close enough, he could take Shore down, but he was too far away and wouldn't risk hitting Bailey by mistake.

"Mason," she cried, but he didn't look at her. He couldn't, or the thin thread holding his control would snap. Instead, he kept his eyes on Shore while slowly sliding from the cart.

"It's over," he told the other man. "Let her go."

"Oh, I think not, *Mason*," Shore sneered, inching toward the plane.

"Come on, Shore," Mason kept his voice light, careful not to let his fear, or his fury, show. "You really think you're going to get away with this? I thought you were smarter than that."

"Mason, look out!"

Mason turned, spotted the new threat and fired. The Butcher's enormous body crumpled and rolled down the steps of the plane to the tarmac, a pool of red surrounding him in seconds.

A flash of heat whizzed past Mason's head, and he hit the ground and rolled, ducking behind the luggage cart. Shore took advantage and edged closer to the plane, Bailey still clutched in front of him. Mason spied Kate at the entrance to the plane, and fired, but the bullet reflected off the door.

Bailey's heart beat in triple time. She struggled to recall what Mason had taught her, but her insides were shaking. Shore was dragging her closer to the plane, and if she didn't do something, they were going to get away. If only she could get her hand on his gun, she might be able to stop him from shooting Mason.

Move his mind.

Mason's words penetrated the panic threatening to engulf her. Shore's attention would be on Mason's gun. She had to shift his concentration from the gun so she could escape. As long as he held her, she knew there was no way Mason would risk firing and hitting her by mistake.

Move his mind.

Reaching into the pocket of her sweatshirt, she pulled the disk from its hiding place and held it out in front of her. "Mason," she called, and flicked her wrist, sending the disk across the tarmac like a Frisbee. "It's his accounts," she yelled, guessing at what the disk really contained. "It has everything you need."

Shore reached for her arm, and she took the advantage, cupping her hand and swinging back for all she was worth, striking her target with amazing accuracy.

Shore buckled forward with a howl of pain. She grabbed the muzzle of the gun, pushing it downward. She felt heat from the report of the weapon against her hand seconds before searing pain and fire gripped her body.

Fury driving him, Mason charged forward when Bailey slipped to the ground unconscious. Using his shoulder, he caught Shore in the midsection. They hit the pavement and Shore's head smacked against the concrete, knocking him cold. Mason slipped a pair of cuffs from his hip pocket and tightened them around Shore's wrists.

He heard a soft click, then felt the cold press of metal against his temple. "You shouldn't have done that, O'Neill," Kate said in a steady voice. "Now I'm going to have to kill you."

"How much was he paying, Morgan?" O'Neill asked. He looked past Shore to Bailey and the pool of red spilling onto the tarmac. He looked closely, searching, praying for a sign she was merely wounded and not… He couldn't bring himself to think of the alternative. If he did, he'd lose it, and could end up getting them all killed.

"Get up, O'Neill. Real slow."

He stood, keeping his eyes on Bailey. She was breathing, and for now he had to take comfort in that fact. Slowly stepping over Shore, he turned to face Kate. Behind her, in the distance, he saw the red lights of at least half a dozen patrol cars speeding across the tarmac.

"It was you all along," he said, hoping to keep her attention. "You were good, Kate. No one knew you were the one who kept feeding Shore information. You had us all fooled."

"Shut up!"

He inched toward her, waiting for an opening. "You and Shore must have had a good laugh all this time. But tell me, Kate. How does it feel to know you killed one of your own?"

"I didn't kill Evers. You're not going to pin that on me."

"You might not have pulled the trigger, but a conspiracy charge will stick. I'll make sure of it, if it's the last thing I do, Kate."

Behind him, Shore groaned. Kate's gaze slid from him to Shore. Everything he'd ever been taught by his mother or the nuns at Saint Agnes Academy flew out the window when he brought back his fist and clipped Kate on the jaw.

She staggered back and he rushed her. Taking the gun from her was easy.

He signaled to the other officers, who moved in

with swift efficiency. "I should just kill you," Mason said, his voice dripping with venom. "But the thought of what those women prisoners will do to a cop sharing their jail space is just too damn appealing."

"Go to hell, O'Neill," she snapped.

"Thanks, but I've already been there," he said, then rushed to Bailey's side as one of the uniformed officers cuffed Kate.

Cops were everywhere, gently guiding the girls from the plane, stuffing Kate and Devlin Shore into patrol cars.

Mason dropped to his knees, carefully cradling Bailey's head in his lap. He gently smoothed the hair away from her face, his heart clenching painfully in his chest. God, she was so pale. "Sweetheart, talk to me," he whispered.

Except for the steady rise and fall of her chest, she lay lifeless in his arms. A hand rested on his shoulder, but he ignored it. Bailey was his only concern. He couldn't lose her. She was his life, and he hadn't even been able to tell her how much he loved her.

"Let the paramedics do their job, partner."

"I'm not leaving her."

"I know, buddy," Blake said. "I know."

Mason squeezed his eyes shut, but the pain wouldn't subside. He felt as if someone had ripped his heart out of his chest with painfully sharp teeth. "She can't die," he choked out.

Blake signaled for the paramedics. "She won't die, Mason. She's been shot, but you have to let them take care of her now. She's lost a lot of blood."

The EMTs approached, then knelt beside Bailey.

Slowly, Mason stood and allowed Blake to move him out of the way so they could stabilize her before transporting her to the closest hospital.

"Here," Blake said, extending his hand and opening his palm. "You left this behind."

Mason stared at the badge. All his life, all he'd ever wanted to be was a cop, just like has dad and granddad. For too many years, he'd put the job before the most important people in his life. Today, he'd put the woman he loved first. Maybe with Bailey's help, he'd learn how to make room in his life for both.

"Thanks," he said, pocketing the shield. "Partner."

BAILEY OPENED her eyes, her gaze resting on O'Neill. He stood by the hospital window, staring out into the night sky. His hands were shoved in the deep pockets of his jeans, his shoulders slumped forward. He looked exhausted and in desperate need of sleep. It had been a rough couple of days.

"Hey there, handsome," she whispered. Her throat ached from the tube they'd shoved down her prior to surgery. When she'd wrestled Shore for the gun, she'd been shot at such close range, the bullet had practically shattered her femur. The doctors assured her she would have no residual effects, but her days of chasing bad guys were definitely over. To be perfectly honest, she looked forward to retirement.

Mason turned and smiled, his honey-colored eyes filling with warmth and tenderness. He neared the bed and sat on the edge, lifting her hand to his lips. "Hey yourself, gorgeous. How you feeling?"

"Like I was shot," she said, her scratchy voice the envy of bullfrogs. She took great comfort in knowing the people responsible were facing a lifetime behind bars. "Where's Les?"

"With your mom and stepdad," he said. "They've been waiting out in the hall to see you."

Her sister was safe and would be heading home to Whitewater with her parents soon. Leslie would need some counseling, not only because of the trauma she'd suffered at the hands of Devlin Shore and his cronies, but also to learn to cope with her grief over losing their father. Difficult times lay ahead for Leslie, but Bailey was confident her sister's newfound maturity, and the love and adoration of her mother and Ned, would see her through the rough patches.

As far as her own life was concerned, Bailey knew only one thing—she planned to spend it with her own surly detective. He hadn't told her he loved her, but she knew the truth. It had been in his eyes when he'd seen her with Shore. It had been in his voice when she'd managed to talk to him on the phone for those few moments before she'd been discovered. And it had been in his heart when he'd made love to her.

She tried to sit up, but the full leg cast made movement difficult. "Darn, no mattress Olympics for a while," she complained good-naturedly. "Whatever are we going to do to pass the time?"

He smiled, a wickedly handsome grin that turned her insides to butter. "I'm sure we'll think of something," he said, then helped her into a more comfortable position before bracing his arms against the mattress and surrounding her with his body.

She returned his grin and wreathed her arms around his neck. "You saying you plan on entertaining me while I'm recuperating, O'Neill?"

He planted a quick, hard kiss on her lips. "I've given it some thought."

She pulled him closer, her lips inches from his. "Oh, you have, huh?"

"Yeah, I have," he said, the teasing light disappearing from his eyes. "I thought I'd lost you, Bailey. I went a little crazy."

"Just a little?" she teased, not wanting the light, easy conversation to end. She liked the lighter side of O'Neill, but loved all of him, every intense, cranky, surly inch.

He frowned deeply. "Okay, a lot," he complained, straightening. He stood and started pacing the hospital room like a caged animal. She took pity on him, knowing how much it cost him to express his emotions. For so long he'd kept things bottled up inside. Perhaps now that he'd finally apprehended Shore, he could lay the past, and his own guilt, to rest.

He stopped and turned, planting his hands on his hips, the deep frown firmly in place. "Look, I know you want to be near your sister, but we can work something out. She can live with us, if that's what it'll take to get you to marry me and move to Chicago. I don't care. But I'm not losing you again, Bailey."

She gazed at him, her heart full of emotion and love. "My sister is going home with my parents."

Her calm tone belied the excitement she was feeling. "She'll see a therapist and eventually pull her life back together. She can visit us when school's out during the summer."

"But I thought—"

"That I'd be so filled with guilt that I'd move back to the farm and forget about the man I want to spend the rest of my life with?" At his nod, she smiled. "Not a chance, O'Neill. I do wish I'd been there for Leslie after our father's death, but my sister made a mistake, and it's not my responsibility to do penance because of it. She loved our dad and has had a hard time adjusting to Mom's new husband, but Ned loves her like she was his own daughter. They'll work it out, and if Leslie wants to visit us, that's great, but she's going home where she belongs."

He neared the bed and sat, taking both of her hands in his. "You're sure? Chicago's not all that far away from Wisconsin, so if you really wanted to live there, we could arrange something. But I want to be near my son, Bailey. I've missed too much of his life already."

"I'm sure," she said, slipping her arms around him and pulling him close. "I'd live on the moon so long as we could be together. And Cody needs you, just as much as you need him."

He trailed the back of his hand along her cheek, his eyes filling with tenderness and love. "I love you, Bailey."

She smiled, one of those secret woman smiles that made him crazy. "That's what I've been trying to tell you all along, O'Neill."

He chuckled, then took her mouth, gently at first, then deep and bone-melting, stealing her breath away. Just the way he'd stolen her heart and her soul.

_____Epilogue_____

"WHAT DO YOU MEAN a 5.4? That was a 6.0, and not a fraction less, O'Neill."

Mason laughed at his wife's feigned outrage. "Don't be so hard on yourself, sweetheart. You just need to get a little more training time in after your injury."

"I'll give you training," she muttered, gliding her body over his in a way that had him gritting his teeth to suppress the groan building in his throat. He lost the battle the minute her tongue wove a path down his chest and over his stomach....

Hours later, they emerged from the bungalow to take a stroll along the white-sand beach of the Jamaican resort to watch the sunrise on the last day of their honeymoon. For ten glorious days, Bailey had been his alone, and although he looked forward to returning to Chicago to spend time with Cody and settle back into the Chicago P.D., he hated the idea of the real world intruding on their lives.

"What are you thinking about?" she asked, guiding him toward a large piece of driftwood that had washed up on the shore.

He sat and tugged her hand until she sat beside him. "That I wish we had another ten days before we had to go home," he admitted, slipping his arm around her.

She leaned against him, laying her head against his shoulder. He loved the feel of her in his arms, and knew he'd never tire of her body pressed against his. Since the day eight months ago when he thought he'd lost her forever, he swore he'd never take a moment with her for granted. So far, he'd kept his word.

For too long he'd put the job first, but now that Shore and Kate Morgan were behind bars, those days were behind him. The deaths of Jim Evers and Ashley Adams were forever imprinted on his memory, but nearly losing Bailey had taught him a valuable lesson about the important things in life. And he planned never to lose sight of those things again, particularly his wife and son.

Bailey had fallen head over heels for Cody, and while his son had been a little hesitant with his new stepmother initially, a bond had been formed that Mason was sure would remain unbreakable. Bailey had been patient, waiting for Cody to come around, and the boy hadn't disappointed her.

She lifted her head and looked at him. "We could stay here," she suggested.

"How would we live?"

The look in her eyes was pure sin, and heated his blood.

He chuckled. "Let me rephrase the question. How would we survive? I've got a while before I'm eligible for my pension."

She pursed her lips, giving the idea some thought. "How about if we hang out a shingle and open a private investigation firm on the island?"

He shook his head. "No way."

"Sure, O'Neill. Listen. We could make this work. We already know we work great together, and—"

He laughed. "Not a chance, Bailey." He couldn't keep her locked up and clothed in cotton batting to protect her, but no way was he ever going to put her in the path of danger again. Once had been enough to last him a lifetime.

She grinned and her eyes sparkled with mischief. "Of course, I'd take care of the books, but I can help with the surveillance. We could—"

He planted a hard kiss on her lips. "Forget it, Mrs. O'Neill."

She shook her head in mock dismay. "You're being stubborn again. I thought we had a talk about that."

He stood and pulled her to her feet and into his arms. Running his hands in gentle sweeps down her back, he kissed her long and hard. She sighed and leaned against him, making him want to forget the sunrise and carry her back to the bungalow they'd called home for the past ten days.

Life with Bailey would never become boring, he thought when he lifted his head and looked into her eyes. The love she'd never been afraid to show him burned brightly within her gaze. His chest constricted with emotion, but he no longer hid from the way Bailey made him feel. Instead, he reveled in the emotions, and in her love.

"I love you, Bailey," he whispered, then captured her mouth for another searing kiss.

Moments later, he ended the kiss and turned her so they were facing the breaking dawn. Together they watched the rainbow of colors shift from predawn gray to a morning sky as blue and clear as his wife's eyes.

As the sun crept over the horizon of the island paradise, Mason held the woman he loved in his arms, and looked forward to tens of thousands of sunrises with her by his side.